POST MAGIC

Ellis Logan

An Earth Lodge® Publication
Roxbury, Connecticut

Published in the U.S.A. by Earth Lodge®
Cover Design by Maya Cointreau

ISBN 978-1-944396-65-7

Every day is a journey, and the journey itself is home.

\- Matsuo Bashō

CHAPTER 1

warm wilds drowsing
last in a string of planets
stars carry magic

Under the dark light of an iridescent sky, the mountain seemed to slumber. There would be no sunrise, for this was a world among stars and dust, lit only by the swirling gases of dueling nebulae. Dark, yet warm; heated by cosmic winds and a fiery interior. Far from the trail, out of sight and sheltered among trees, I tamped out the last flames of my cooking fire and reached out to the ether to call up a small quelling breeze, a whisper of air to disperse the smoke among the canopy above.

The fire had been a necessary evil, a way to sear the brook trout I'd netted upon waking an hour ago, but I preferred not to be caught alone in the wilds if I could help it. And I could always help it. The night before, I had camped far off the trail among a copse of trees and set wards of warning along the perimeter. Friendly wanderers were less common these days than roving thieves.

The planet Renga was home to an increasingly diverse population: descendants of original settlers, mostly of miner descent like me; billionaire tycoons bent on earning (or buying) a fiefdom; bandits; anti-tech health nuts; and other fringe groups lured by the planet's off-grid reality. A lack of tech persisted naturally here. The same elements that had made the mining so profitable here five hundred years ago also held electromagnetic properties that made it almost impossible for modern tech to thrive. Even the most rudimentary computing device would stop working within days, sometimes hours. In many ways, Renga was like a living museum. Old-timey gadgets that should have gone the way of the dinosaurs still commanded a thriving market here, machines deemed ancient and barbaric by most galactic standards were coveted and valuable.

Which of course is why anyone hiding from the Peoples Galactic Confederation authorities thought Renga was just peachy. The planet also attracted its fair share of third and fourth sons, billionaire prospectors aiming for feudal lordships. The governmental system here varied widely by locale: galactic, feudal, republican. In some places, it was a free for all.

I'd never known anything better or more modern – found it hard to imagine there even was such a thing. Renga was my home. My family had been among the planet's first settlers. Japanerican miners, born and bred. They'd set up shop above the largest deposit of Chaline in the known galaxy, a pricey clay-like substance used by medics to nourish the body, reverse the aging process and trigger deep healing. You can imagine the demand: everyone wanted it, yet few could afford it.

The first settlement, Puraimura, had blossomed over the years to hold the honorary title of capital city according to the Peoples Galactic Confederation. If the rest of the planet didn't quite agree anymore, well, that wasn't any concern of the Republic. Most people these days called it Prime City, or just Prime for short. Me? I called it home.

I stood up, dusting off my coat and shaking out the knit silken fibers. Leaves tended to cling to the ankle-length jacket, but I loved it. The dark blue yarn was interwoven with a pattern of off-color leaves, naturally cloaking my presence when I traveled the wilds. As a special courier for the Peoples Galactic Postal Service, I had drawn the attention of more than one bandit in the past. Despite my slight frame, I could hold my own and was proud to say I'd never lost a single missive. I was faster and stronger than most, and I could run for hours without stopping. Still, it was better to avoid trouble if I could.

It wasn't only bandits I had to worry about. Not everyone was so accepting of GMO chimeras like me. Kems, for short. Here, they called us kets, which was accurate enough. My people had been genetically modified with panther DNA and a few other minor additions that made us hardier and more suited for the dark mines of Renga and its surface. When they'd first come, the atmosphere hadn't been ameliorated yet, oxygen levels were still low, and the surface had yet to be inoculated with earth bio-forms. For over a hundred years, most of the miners had lived out their days under a cluster of hard-shelled domes working the mines, while the engineers worked on terraforming the planet. Gene tweaks helped my ancestors see in the dark, sense disturbances in the mines, and detect and manage safety issues more easily when they were topside. Enhanced reflexes and agility were key to their survival, especially when an unstable section of mines collapsed in 2487. But the same energy waves that made it so hard to use tech here triggered some other changes in our DNA, made us more in tune with the quantum field of this planet. Some people said what we could do was just physics, masquerading as the unexplained – others called it magic. And, despite what you might have thought, not everyone liked it.

Some people here believed magic sinful. Others sought ways to use it to their advantage. And then there were the purists: people who considered my modified DNA tainted, unsightly or plain demonic. You would have thought in a Galactic Confederation of literally thousands of worlds that people would have seen it all. I mean, we'd found other life in the universe, other races of intelligent beings, some humanoid, some not. Creatures with barely any bodies at all, mere whispers of energy, like rainbows of sound and light and song. Treaties had been made, a few wars fought. There were planets where races converged, trading hubs where everyone lived together in peace, lawless pirate planets where no governments ruled. But it wasn't the norm.

Mostly, the different species stayed out of each other's way, sticking to their own sectors of the galaxy. Different habitat requirements tended to make it easier that way. Certainly, there was space enough.

The separation did nothing to ease racial discrimination, though. Some people went so far as to liken kems to aliens, fearful that our modifications made it harder to tell who was who.

So, yeah. I was no stranger to prejudice. It didn't bother me – much. But it was as good an excuse as any to live among my own people in Prime. I didn't have much family left, so as a twentieth-generation descendent of the original settlers, it was comforting to stick close to my roots. Too bad my brother didn't feel the same way.

Stooping, I picked up the small stick I'd been carving and turned it over in my fingers a few times, finding the sensation of the smooth, etched wood pressing against my skin comforting. I shouldered my pack, wishing I didn't miss him so much. I hadn't seen Jonah in over a year. He'd rebuffed my proposal to share the New Year's meal three months ago, declined my invitation to a birthday party the year before. We hadn't been close for years. Maybe it was time to let it go. I had plenty of friends and cousins back home. So what if my twin wanted to pretend I didn't exist?

My ears twitched, the way they always did when I was annoyed, and I ruffled the hair between them, more out of habit than any actual desire to be presentable. Prime was only a few hours walk away, just a quick descent down the mountain. If I'd been sticking to the main route through my delivery sector it would be quite a bit longer, but I rarely did anything the way you'd expect. My grandfather had often regaled me with tales of his misspent youth, the years he'd wandered throughout the wilds of Renga delivering mail before he'd settled down with my grandmother. It was his bag that I carried today, a well-worn leather pack that generations of post runners had used before me. My grandfather had insisted it came from First Earth itself, a true relic of the past, but I doubted the leather could possibly be that old. Still, I cared for it regularly, carefully cleaning and oiling the leather after every run, exactly the way my jiji had done.

It was also he, Onkoro Wakanazu, who had ingrained in me the importance of staying off the beaten path, far away from the preying eyes and devilish snares of any would-be bandits.

"Nikta, you must always be strong. Not just in body, but in mind," he used to remind me, tapping his forehead. "The weak get eaten by the strongest. Survival of the fittest is no antiquated scientific principle, not here on Renga."

The memory of Jiji made me think of home and I became anxious to return. I broke into an easy run, my woven boots flexing with each stride, hitting the forest floor soundlessly. I didn't only have ears like a cat – I could run like one, too. Graceful, silent and dangerously fast on my feet. As I ran, a grating screech tore through the forest and a small reddish shape missed my face by inches. An owl. Wings soundless in flight, it was perhaps the only occupant of the forest quieter than me today. Squeaks pierced the night when the owl found its prey, talons securing the small vole in its grasp as it flew up into one of the nearby trees. I wasn't fazed, familiar as I was with the circle of life. Life on Renga wasn't always easy. If you didn't watch out for yourself, nobody else would. *Weak meat, strong eat*, I thought. I had always enjoyed that simple truth, considering it fair enough.

The vole, of course, would not have agreed.

CHAPTER 2

*left behind - chimeras rise
to lonely foster, heat, rains*

Running and leaping fearlessly through gaps in the trees all the way down the mountain cut my transit time in half and soon I found myself walking through the outskirts of Puraimura. The first settlement of Renga, this city had definitely seen better days. Like so many places before it that centered their existence around one particular good or product, when that good ran out, the economy suffered. And, again like so many other cities, when the economy suffered those with vision did not suffer to stay and improve the home they knew. No, when the chaline ran dry our visionaries had moved on, creating gorgeous citadels like Chalinex and planned communities like The Fringe, or they had shipped off-planet entirely, searching for brighter pastures.

My vision was as good as anyone else's but I had no plans to leave Prime City. Maybe the architecture was a bit dated, the art and culture provincial by galactic standards. None of that mattered to me. Prime was my home, not to mention the fact that it was the planetary headquarters for the Peoples Galactic Postal Service, Peoples Post or PGPS for short. Sure, I could work as a runner anywhere on Renga – but Prime was the heart and soul of operations. All off-world mail arrived first in Prime for sorting. You would have thought that physical mail would be a thing of the past, and in most worlds, it was. Like everything else that required computing, here on Renga that sort of communication was out. And, of course, there were always things that needed a softer touch. Messages too sensitive to transmit by galactic frequency. Heirlooms that needed to pass from hand to hand in a reliable fashion. That was where the Peoples Post came in, our bread and butter, so to speak. Mail and other supplies were delivered to the PGPS transfer station on the smallest and closest of our three orbiting moons – Hokku was more of a pebble, really, when you compared it to Sakura and Yuki – and then brought down via specially designed transports. Once sorted, post runners like me handled everything marked "Carry with Care": the most sensitive materials. Everything else moved from city to city in large armored vehicles that ran off the galactic radiation bombarding the planet day-in and day-out. Barely a step above the earliest steam engines, considered archaic by most of the 'verse, the trucks represented some of the best we had to work with.

Even with specially-made heavy shielding, incoming ships from Hokku could only dock for a maximum of six hours. Long enough to unload, refuel, and reload before blasting off toward Hokku again. It was common practice for teens on Renga to visit the station after they graduated school to celebrate and blow off steam, but I'd never been. There had been so much else to do back then. Partying with space hookers and trying my hand at the gaming tables had been the furthest thing from my mind. Though even I had to admit, the pictures my friend Jericha had brought back had been epic.

Right now, the grey orb of the small moon hung low in the sky above. Since the only sun in our solar system was so far away it appeared as a mere pinprick in the sky, we based our days on Hokku's twenty-six-hour orbit. As it rose, morning began, first hour. Most schools and businesses opened at two. By the time Hokku's pale blue orb set at the thirteenth hour, most offices had already been closed a few hours and evening began. At least, that is what our clocks told us.

In reality, our sky was an ever-shifting tapestry of nebulae, gases and dust swirling in a cacophony of color, never truly dark. Despite our distance from the central sun, the planet never cooled, warmed instead by the radiation of the nebulae and a molten core. We had the best hot springs in the 'verse and a fantastic team of Olympic swimmers. No chimeras allowed, of course. That last bit had broken my brother's heart. He'd been the best swimmer at our high school, but the scouts had passed him over for the totally human, absolutely non-GMO third string slacker. In other words, a regular human, or reg for short. After that, Jonah had just sort of shut down. He'd stopped talking to me, both at school and at home. After our mama died and Jiji had gotten sick, he'd run off to Chalinex, leaving me to take care of Jiji all by myself. Not that I'd minded that part of it. It just... well, if I was honest it still hurt. I missed him. We'd always been a pair, even if we weren't identical. Without him, I felt like a spare chopstick.

"Nikta, heya!" A familiar voice grabbed my attention, and I looked up, spotting its owner. Maury Lew was waving from his vendor window overlooking the street, a plate of steaming hot buns on a tray in front of him. Eager, I rushed to say hello, giving him a slight bow.

"Heya, Maury. How are you today?"

"I'm good, Nikta, can't complain." He glanced quickly over his shoulder, then dropped his voice to a conspiratorial whisper. "Actually, it's Maeve's birthday tonight, think you can make it over for the party? It's a surprise."

"A surprise? Didn't she give you a black eye the last time you tried to surprise her?" I asked, picking up one of the buns he had pushed towards me and biting into the sweet, soft dough.

"That was an accident. We surprised her a little too much. Trust me. This time's gonna be great."

"Alright. If you think you're up to it," I said, grinning. "What can I bring?"

Maury's dark eyes took in my dusty clothes. "You coming off a run?"

I nodded. "Yep, on my way to the office now. But I should have plenty of time to get ready, if that's what you're worried about."

"You should rest more," he said, eyeing me critically. Maeve had gone to school with my mother, and I'd been coming to their noodle shop for as long as I could remember. "Onkoro would not want to see you working so hard. Your mother, too, she would-"

I cut him off, not wanting to hear what my mother would have thought. Despite the years that had passed, her death still cut through me like a knife. There had been no warning, no gentle easing into the afterlife as there had been with my jiji. She had simply dropped one day, dead before she hit the floor. A blood clot, the doctors had said. Demons, the superstitious had whispered. Either way, it had felt like the end of the world. It didn't matter how much magic I had. There was nothing I could do to bring her back. Even if I had been able to afford a round of chaline for treatment, there wouldn't have been any time. No warning. And, of course, chaline was in short supply these days. Local mines had run out long ago and chaline remained a controlled substance – something you had to apply for, wait for. Unless, of course, you had substantial wealth, something on par with the ownership of a planet. In general, it was reserved for the most dire cases: young children with rare diseases, pregnant mothers, that sort of thing. Older people, simple people like my jiji, they almost never qualified.

So much had changed in that one short year – my mother, Jiji, and Jonah, all gone in their own way. And here I remained, trying to keep it all together, trying to pretend nothing had changed.

"I love my work," I insisted, smiling as I stole another bun and danced backwards towards the street. "Even more than these buns. What time is the party?"

"Twelve," Maury shouted after me. "Don't be late!"

"I won't!" I yelled, then stuffed the rest of the bun into my mouth and dashed between bodies in the oncoming crowd. It was already past eight. If I wanted to get cleaned up, find a gift and make the party, there was no time to waste. "Lew's Noos" was still about twenty blocks away from the postal depot. I pulled my hood up over my face, hoping to avoid idle chit chat with acquaintances in the street. Still, the fragrant market stalls assaulted my senses and I couldn't help stopping for a few more savory treats along the way. This time, I kept the conversations short and paid my way in yendars.

Finally, I made it to the post office. Being a courier, I didn't use the front door but slipped into a side alley that led around to the back of the building. I took out my trio of keys crafted of brass, bronze, and steel and set to unlocking the three impressive tumblers. Mail was serious business and the PGPS wasn't about to let just anyone get their hands on it. Inside the door, a locked gate presented another barrier. My hood was still up but the guard behind the bars recognized me without even looking.

"Heya, Nikta," he drawled, slowly marking his place in the comic he'd been reading before standing to let me through. The gate could only be opened from the inside, so there was always a guard on duty, even in the dead of night.

"Hey Joe," I smiled, drawing the hood back. "How did you know it was me?"

"Those old boots of yours are a dead giveaway, plus, you know, your scent."

I wrinkled my nose. "Is it that bad?" I hadn't showered since the morning before, I knew, and I had been sticking to a pretty fast pace.

"You kidding me? You smell like flowers, doesn't matter what you do. Nothing in the 'verse can wash that off or cover it up. Not from me, at any rate."

I blushed. No one had ever mentioned my underscent before, at least, not out of the bedroom. The few times they had, I'd chalked it up to pillow talk, not an accurate assessment of my olfactory appeal. Like me, Joe was a chimera. He didn't have much magic but his sense of smell was off the charts. The PGPS usually employed him in the customs department making sure there weren't any dangerous substances passing through. It was strange to see him here reading by the door, and I told him so.

He scratched behind his neck absently. "Yeah, I know but Berman is off duty with food poisoning or something. She's been puking for two days straight, her wife called in for her sounding pretty out of it herself."

"Wow, that sucks for both of them."

"Tell me about it."

"Alright, well, see you later. Hope you brought plenty of comics."

"I'm already on my second read through with this one," he said, fingering the pages. "I forgot how much I hated gate duty. I can't wait to get back to the customs department. You got anything to read in that pack of yours?" he asked hopefully.

"Nothing I can part with," I said, thinking of my tiny booklet of Bashō's collected poetry. "Sorry."

"No problem, just had to ask." He yawned. "I'm off in an hour."

I nodded absently, remembering that I was on a timeline.

"'Kay, see you around." I headed straight to the receiving department. When I reached Florence's massive table I started pulling out letters and packages, carefully arranging them so that none of the reusable mail cylinders rolled away. The tables at the PGPS had raised edges to keep things from sliding off, but it still paid to be careful. "Here you go: here's everything I collected."

"Nikta," she purred. "I was starting to worry. We were expecting you in last night."

"I know, sorry, Flo. I had to make a delivery at Herold farm, you know how that goes," I said. Mrs. Herold was a widowed homesteader whose son had run off to Hokku the year before. Even when she'd had family near, she'd been notorious among runners for her predilection for talking. Now, she'd start preparing tea and fresh rice cakes the moment she heard you coming down her lane. Most people found it impossible to get out of there in less than a day, though I had reduced it to an art form, generally managing to get out in under three hours without hurting her feelings.

"Ah, yes, Mrs. Herold," she said gently. Florence was in her sixties, working a cushy job these days, but she'd started as a runner like the rest of us. "How is she doing?

"Better now. Not so lonely since she hired a farmhand to take up the work the men used to do."

"No other trouble?" she asked, cocking an eyebrow. "How'd you find the roads? I heard Route 8 got washed out in the last storm."

"No idea. You know I stick to the wilds as much as possible."

"Oh, well, I thought you might have heard something along the way. I've been getting some weird reports; customers acting strangely. I had two new runners resign on me out of the blue this week, no explanation."

"Really, who?"

"Bobby and Lara," she frowned as if it was my fault. And yeah, okay, I had kind of recruited Bobby. But he'd wanted the job.

"I don't get it. Well, Lara, sure. She didn't seem to have the stamina to be a runner. But Bobby's got a family to feed. He told me he needed the work."

"I know. I thought it was strange, too, but he just gave me some lame excuse about deciding to stay close to home so he could help take care of the family. And after all the training we've been doing these last few weeks... I guess maybe his wife thought he'd be away too much."

"Wow, okay." I chewed my lip, hoping everything was okay with Bobby. Our weeks were long by galactic standards – thirteen days, or half one Renga month. People generally worked two days on, one day off, and enjoyed a two-day weekend at the finish. Runners had no set timetable, though, and our schedules could easily cause some strain at home.

"Yeah," Flo went on, fuming. "So between losing those two and Stephor still being out on paternity leave, we're running short on couriers." She wandered away, motioning for me to follow her to another massive table stacked with mail. The outgoing pile. She was right. We were running short – I'd never seen so much mail stacked and waiting. There were even piles on the floor nearby. "We're splitting up the sectors, everybody's picking up the slack. I've got a bunch of things from Stephor's route that were meant for Bobby, do you think you'll be able to take them out tomorrow? I know you were supposed to be off for a couple of days, but..." she trailed off, waving a hand towards the piles, frustration clearly written across her face along with an apology.

"Sure, no problem. Any chance I can get some extra yendars out of it?" I asked hopefully.

Flo laughed. "You know that's not how it works. You should be glad no one's docking your pay for coming in a day slow and making me worry," she teased. Not that the Peoples Post would ever do that, not here on Renga or anywhere else. Runners worked on salary, a hefty income of Confederation Credits that more than covered all our travels, plus full benefits and a very attractive retirement package. Being paid in credits didn't hurt here on Renga, either, where two ceecees could buy five yendar. In return, the PGPS was able to guarantee deliveries that would arrive ASAP - as soon as possible. No one liked to commit to a deadline in space, not even the PGPS. Our motto had been amended, too, over the years:

"Neither ice nor heat nor stars alight
stays our couriers from the swift completion
of their appointed rounds."

In fact, our ships were so reliable and respected that more than one stowaway had used them to try and sneak into combat zones and other restricted areas. What can I say? The Peoples Post was pretty badass. I liked knowing that I was part of something so big with such a long history. It didn't hurt knowing that we helped keep families connected, either. It was nice to be welcomed wherever I went. The bandits who'd love to get their hands on what I carried? Well, every job had its downsides. I could more than take care of myself, thanks to my grandfather's tutelage. Still, even if Florence wasn't going to dock my pay for being late, I knew she liked to keep track of where her couriers were. As if to prove my point, Flo held up a waterproofed sheet detailing the new sector and travel schedule. "Here you go. There're a lot of new stops on there for you, and a package for some cop over in Chalinex, I figured you'd-"

"Chalinex!" I ripped the paper out of her hands. "Let me see that." I scanned the paper, reading the address. Anywhere else in the galaxy, I'd have been getting a neural uplink with all the information, but not here on Renga. The tech just wasn't compatible with the planet, or my brand of magic. "That's the precinct where Jonah works. This is great! Thank you, Flo!" I threw my arms around her and gave her a giant hug. She laughed and hugged me back.

"Easy kiddo, you're gonna squeeze the life out of me! I wasn't sure if it was the same the precinct, but I know you've been itching to take over some of the Chalinex deliveries."

"Yes, thank you, thank you!"

"Yeah, well, Stephor can't expect to hold onto the best sector forever, not if he's going to keep extending his leave."

"Aw, he can't help it. Have you seen the baby?"

Flo's smile broadened. "I sure have. Kid's a keeper. But, the mail never sleeps. So if you want more Chalinex deliveries, they're yours."

"Definitely! Oh, Flo, you've made my day!" I scooped up my pile of correspondence and small packages and stuffed them into my pack. "Seriously, you're the best."

"That's what I keep saying," she said, smiling. "Now, if you'd head over to Allen in customs and tell him that..."

"Somebody say my name?" Allen said, cutting through the other postmasters' tables with a large cup of tea between his hands. Flo frowned at him and I suppressed a giggle. Allen had been nitpicking Flo's handiwork for over a decade, always asking her to reprint or correct various declaration forms. Personally, I thought it was his socially inadequate way of trying to get her attention.

"Uh-oh, your suitor is here," I whispered in her ear. Flo had other, less polite ways of referring to Allen. She hissed under her breath but I ignored her and turned brightly towards the aging customs officer. "I'm heading out, big plans for the evening. You two have fun! Bye-ie!" I waved at them both and bounced back before Flo could swat me with her talons. She may not have had actual cat's claws, but she kept her nails filed razor sharp, a habit held over from her days as a runner. As long as Allen stayed out of arms reach, I knew he'd be safe. Besides, Flo was all hiss and no bite. I knew she liked to complain about Allen, but I was pretty sure that the mild workplace drama helped keep her from getting too bored at her desk job.

It wasn't easy going from runner to postmaster, though most people made the transition in the years before retirement. Personally, I wasn't sure what I would do when I got there. Somedays, even being a special courier wasn't quite enough. I understood the lure of the stars, of life outside the confines of Renga, because there were days when I felt it, too. Surely, life up there was bigger, grander. I wasn't sure what I wanted out of life, but I knew that I needed to matter. Right now, delivering letters got me there. Kind of. It gave me a greater purpose. But some days, like now, I couldn't help feeling that there had to be something I was missing. Something more.

I just had no idea what that might be.

CHAPTER 3

water moves like blood
when friends are family bound.
Lover! one more time.

Even though I'd been gone for less than a week, the air in my apartment was stale, fetid. I had the entire top floor of a five-story walkup, an open plan flat surrounded by walls of windows. I didn't like to feel cooped up and had moved out of our tiny family dwelling shortly after Jiji had passed. It was one of the nicer things that came with living alone – the ability to completely and utterly think about pleasing only myself.

I plopped my pack down on the large round table that served as office, crafting table and dining surface, then proceeded to check the garbage. As I'd suspected, I'd forgotten to empty the trash before I'd left. Trying not to gag and failing miserably, I tied up the refuse and sent it down the chute out in the hall for composting. Returning to the apartment, I spent the next few minutes opening all the windows – four per side, except for the corner where the bathroom was located behind two half walls, so fifteen in all. I even slid back the small hatch in the middle of the central sky-dome, a gorgeous leaded piece spanning twenty feet of ceiling that had been a deciding factor when I'd signed the ten-year lease.

I'd placed my bed directly under the dome, so much the better for stargazing. The four corners of the apartment spread out from the bed like a compass of living: cooking and dining in one corner, to one side of the door; entertaining and lounging to the other; clothes and bathing next; and finally, my indoor contemplation garden, a jumble of fruit trees, vegetable vines, and some of my favorite medicinal plants and herbs. Gently, I plucked a couple of newly ripened sweet lemons. Everbearing vines climbing up the wall provided several handfuls of golden raspberries, most of which made it into a bowl on the counter for breakfast the next day. The rest I ate on the spot, gazing over the city. Dark clouds to the east smothered the view. Humid air wafted in, carrying the smell of decay outside and replacing it with a hint of ozone. Rain was coming. I'd have to remember to close everything up before I headed out. Renga was warm, just the way I liked it, and it tended to rain every few days, with the largest storms brewing whenever Sakura began to rise. The huge pink moon resembled its namesake, the cherry blossom, in color only. Every twenty-six days it rose on the horizon and as it passed the pull it exerted on the vast ocean to the north was like a siren call to the twin gods, thunder and lightning. We marked the months by its arrival, each new appearance a cause for celebration and joy, a time to dance in the rain.

Sakura had set over several days ago, leaving behind a sodden terrain and clear skies. Regardless of what Joe may have said about my beautiful flowery scent, I was pretty sure the mud and sweat on my skin had ripened.

I rinsed the large obsidian bathtub, inserted the plug and turned the hot water on full blast. It would take about ten minutes for the bath to fill, during which time I used the small shower stall in the corner, hitting a button that delivered a fragrant blend of soap and water to wash over my body. Out in the wilds, I'd neglected the harai, purification and blessing rituals held when Sakura sets. Oh, I'd said a few prayers, rinsed my face in a narrow stream, but I'd hardly nurtured myself as prescribed whenever the gods and ancestors left Renga for a period of holy rest. Now, I could linger and perform the ritual cleansing as I'd been taught. The ancestors wouldn't return till the end of the week; I was sure they wouldn't mind the lateness of my attention to detail. After a thorough scrubbing, I depressed the button, rinsing in the cool clear water that resulted. Not bothering to towel off, I left the stall and lowered myself into the bath, allowing the waters to close in over my shoulders. The warmth and comfort were so blissful, I groaned with satisfaction. Leaning back, I closed my eyes and sank into a pattern of healing deep breaths.

I may have fallen asleep. Despite the stone tubs ability to hold heat, the water had gone cold when I finally opened my eyes again. I climbed out, drawing on my favorite silk kimono, a hand-me-down from my mother. A golden affair decorated along the hem with scarlet carp, it had been designed for a woman taller than I. Now, I allowed the open ends to trail behind me as I walked without tying it closed. I padded through the bamboo-floored apartment, unworried about prying eyes. We may not have had the presence of a central sun on Renga, but the system of nebulas that surrounded us constantly bombarded the planet with a nourishing cocktail of vitamins and galactic frequencies.

If we wanted to stay our healthiest, we needed those rays. Buildings here were built to take advantage of the cosmic buffet, using large one-way glass windows that allowed a person to see outside but no one could spy within. We were a people without curtains. Unless, of course, you were one of the unlucky few who found the low-light glimmerings of the heavens disturbing to their sleep. Some people swore the stars sang to them, whispers of the gods without rest. If I tried really hard, sometimes I imagined I could hear them. My mother had sung to me each night when I was a girl, strange songs she said came from above. But the time for lullabies had passed. Now, I needed something to wake me up.

I filled a dark glass pot with water and set it to simmer on the stove. Then, I harvested some fresh cilantro and lemon verbena and placed them in a small cup. That would reset my clock.

While the water heated, I lit several sandalwood joss sticks, standing them in a bowl of stones I'd placed on a small altar in my garden. A small, framed photo of my parents and grandparents taken on the day of my parents' wedding sat next to the bowl along with several small hand-carved wooden statues: Tara, the goddess of compassion; a fairy with diamonds for eyes; and a winged dragon. Silently, I thanked the spirits for watching over my apartment while I was away and sent love to my family, both dead and living. Then, never one for lingering over my prayers, I rose to check out my closet.

I didn't have a lot of clothes, especially not fancy ones, but this was Maeve's birthday. She was as close to an aunt as I had; she deserved to be celebrated. I pulled out a long sheath made of the softest bamboo fibers. Slits cut razor sharp up the sides towards my hips, a high neck covering my collar bones in the front while the back dipped down into a plunging V. Misty green set off my eyes perfectly. But what to wear for shoes? The boots by the door wouldn't do. Joe had been right – they were in serious need of cleaning, something I would treat them to the following morning at Pepe's Pedicurie. Looking over the options in my closet, I decided some basic sandals would do. It wasn't like I'd be wearing the shoes indoors. Only an off-worlder would wear their shoes inside, tracking dirt through their host's home. If I tried to wear my shoes indoors, Maeve would likely beat me over the head with a bottle of peach wine, even if it was her favorite.

I rimmed my eyes with kohl, same as I usual. I wasn't too inventive when it came to a beauty routine. I spent some extra time on my hair, making sure the fine mane of honey and cinnamon was perfectly spiked, sticking up between the blackened ears on the top of my head. I could have grown my hair in any style, but I liked to keep it fuss-free. Plus, it reminded me of some pictures I'd seen of an extinct species from First Earth. The article had said that humans had long believed that hyenas were vicious creatures, but in their final days it had been discovered that they were in fact a strong knit maternal society that cared for its young and could stand up to larger predators like lions. Like them, I was small of frame but fierce when it came to family, and the cut pleased me.

I'd lost a good chunk of the evening already, dozing off in the bath. By the time I arrived at the Lewis's the festivities were in full swing. Most people were coming off of a long day's work and they were ready to party hard. I was just glad to see the faces my friends and smell food that I hadn't roasted over an open fire pit or gutted myself. When I was in the wilds, I ate plenty of fish and foraged greens. Sometimes, I even fasted, which was supposedly good for the body and soul but generally made me meaner than a fistful of nettles. When I was home, I stuck to the finer things. Sticky buns, mochi, slow-roasted pork and bowls of berries.

Leaving my shoes in the hall, I slipped inside the open door and took a moment to soak it all in. A young girl sang in the corner, a haunting tune that spoke of moss and smoke. Maeve spotted me, put down a crate of wine on the counter and rushed forward to envelop me in a long hug. It felt so warm, so comforting, I admit I purred a little. Contact was a premium among my kind. Kets didn't groom each other, despite what some of the regs liked to say, but we did enjoy physical contact and tended to be more demonstrative than our full-fledged human cousins once we got to know you. Until then, many of us might have seemed stand-offish as we waited to see if you were worth our notice.

"Glad you could make it," Maeve said looking me over. "You look well, but skinny. Are you getting enough to eat when you're out there in the wild?"

I laughed. "I'll always be skinny, you know that. And you're one to talk," I said, swatting her small frame. "What's your excuse?"

Her face clouded over. "Actually, I've been having a hard time sleeping. Jimmy hasn't been around in weeks, won't return our calls. I don't know what's going on with him." Jimmy was Maeve and Maury's youngest son, and he'd always been a little wild. Even though he'd been a couple years behind me in school, he'd run with kids in my grade. I'd tried to keep an eye on him back then, but we'd had different interests. Now? I'd heard he'd been playing errand boy for a group of homesteaders outside of town, but I wasn't sure which one.

"I'm sorry. Anything I can do?"

She shook her head, frowning. "I don't think so." She forced a smile. "Maybe he'll show up tonight. The night's still young. Maury sent him an invitation last week."

I held back any scathing commentary I might have made about how a son ought not need reminding on his mother's birthday. If my mother had still been alive today… well, nothing could have kept me from seeing her.

"Well, you have me," I said instead. "And you know what, I'm actually pretty damn hungry. How about pointing me in the direction of the food?"

"I'll do better than that. I'll take you myself."

Maeve linked arms with me, bearing me through the crowd the way I'd seen her walk with my mother so many times in my youth. Like I was her prized possession, a jewel to be proud of. They had been so close, Maeve and my mother. But for all the love between us, I hadn't been around much. I couldn't be around her without remembering Ma, and sometimes, it hurt. In the end, as much as Maeve may have prized my presence, she failed in her goal of delivering me to the food. There were so many people wanting to greet her, she finally gave up, shooing me on while she succumbed to the small talk. I understood; she was, after all, the guest of honor. Besides, their home was not so large that I couldn't guess where the food might be. I'd already ruled out the living room and dining room, which left the kitchen or the garden balconies. The Lewises had a massive series of decks where they grew many of their own ingredients. I should have guessed that the food would be here. I just hadn't realized it would be all the food in Prime.

In a gluttonous presentation of overabundance, four massive rectangular tables sagged under the weight of bounty, huge pillar candles lighting the display. The first held sweet sticky rice balls and savory pastries.

The second, smoked fish and slow roasted meats. The third was piled high with fresh fruits and brilliant salad mixtures, and the last, my favorite, was an intoxicating collection of sweets centered around one glorious four-story cake. I groaned. This. Was. Heaven.

"I remember the last time you made that sound." The deep voice sent shivers down my spine, but I played it cool, turning around slowly like I had all the time in the world.

"What makes you think that was the last time?" I blinked calmly up into the dark eyes of Innis McRory. Six feet of simmering strength stared down at me.

"Wasn't it?" Maeve's nephew asked huskily, undaunted.

"Not quite," I said plainly. I hadn't seen Innis in over a month.

He pressed up against me. "Well, how about the best time?"

I cocked an eyebrow, staring up at him. Considering. I let the seconds tick by. Finally, I answered. "Meh. You're okay." Truth was, he was fantastic, but I'd never let him know it. Five minutes after fantastic, he'd be wanting me to stay home, play house, have kittens.

I wasn't ready for any of it. I missed having my family around, but that didn't mean I was ready to breed a new one. I liked my freedom, liked living alone, liked not having to answer to anyone. I didn't need any new relationships. I just wanted to repair the ones I had.

Sleeping with Innis always felt like a mistake. I knew better than to get my sugar and my bread at the same shop. Trouble was, he was just so damned tempting. I extricated myself from his arms and turned back to the tables of food.

"This is amazing, isn't it?" I asked, changing the conversation. "Have you ever seen so much delicious food in one place?"

"I've seen you," he whispered in my ear and I blushed. By Kwan Yin's good graces, he couldn't see my face. Did I mention the man was relentless? This was how he had convinced me to go home with him in the first place, despite my misgivings.

"Shh," I warned. "This is a family affair, behave." I removed his hands from my waist and stepped forward, picking up a plate. "If you want to make yourself useful, go grab a plate of those meat rolls. I haven't had real food in days."

He sighed but complied, heading over to the far table. Relieved, I started loading my own plate with fresh mangos and strawberries, and several delectable pink mochi balls for good measure. I'd scarcely finished before he was back, herding me towards the far end of the balcony where vines screened in a small pergola. I smiled, placing my plate down on the small table, ready to sit.

I never got the chance.

Innis spun me in his arms, cradling me even as he directed me around the corner of the deck and his lips crashed into mine. And again, despite my intentions, I moaned. Those strong, amazing arms of his got me every time. Now, I ran my hands over the muscles that corded their length and smiled into him. Screw the rules. If Innis wanted to play with fire, let him. He was a big boy.

So when he hoisted me up, I only took a moment to make sure no one could see us. We were on an empty stretch of decking, shielded from everything and everyone. Vowing to keep silent, I gave myself over to enjoying the moment. Still, I knew I had to be fair. Had to warn him.

"This doesn't mean anything. I'm not looking for a relationship. I told you before."

"So you've said," he said, hands roving over my body, pinning me against the brick wall.

Which of course, didn't mean anything, didn't mean he'd really *heard* me. But did I even care, when his lips were praying over my body like the most hallowed of temples?

"Five minutes, McRory," I gasped. "You have five minutes."

"I can work with that."

CHAPTER 4

strange solitude breeds complaint
slime wants to slither and slide

Buddha's bodhi tree, that boy could work it. Four minutes of heaven had left my body singing and primed for more. McRory would have been happy to go for another round, gods knew he could perform, but I'd kept him to his promise and insisted on returning to the party and staying under Maeve's radar. It was her night – I wasn't about to ruin it. Innis was her favorite nephew and if she thought we were dating she'd be over the moons. I didn't want to have to correct her. I had ducked out of the party as soon as I thought I could, citing an early morning and a courier's duty.

Which brought me here. Covered in road dust yet again. My favorite kind of dirt. Better than sex, better than berries. Hitting the third stop on the new route, a place I'd never been before. A place far from any path, deep in desert boulderlands, a place where few settled. I'd checked the coordinates three times to be sure I was headed to the right place, stocked up on fish before I left the wilds. Who knew if there'd be anything to forage where I was going – it was a region I'd only ventured into three or four times in my life, each time on survival training runs with Jiji and Jonah. Each time, my mother had wrung her hands, worried we wouldn't return.

Yet here I was. I'd had to scramble down a steep incline of rubble and boulders, stone giants heaped on top of each other, just to get to the odd isolated fortress nestled among the toes of an abandoned quarry. So much for my nice clean boots. Pepe would be dismayed to know I'd already ruined his handiwork. I didn't know how anyone had even managed to build this place, unless there was some sort of hidden access road I couldn't see. It was almost as if someone had used explosives to destroy the way, but who would do that? It wasn't the strangest place that I'd ever been, but it definitely made the top ten.

Straightening my pack and squaring my shoulders, I approached what seemed to be the only door. Unlike most buildings on Renga, there were no windows, no glass ceilings or ways to get in. Only the door. I hoped the occupants were into star-bathing or had some good sun-lights inside, or else they weren't going to stay healthy long. Not that it was my concern. Besides, a place like this, so isolated, had to have its own food production system. No way they were bringing in supplies down that boulder field I'd just navigated.

The fortress was sunk into the cliffs behind it, with what I guessed to be only a small portion of its face visible. I wondered what sort of people had made their home here – religious fanatics? Bandits? Some paranoid rich person? I was about to find out. The building was built from the same stones that lay in ruin around it, amalgamations of dark basalt and vermillion rhyolite. The titanium door had to be custom made, shiny and newly minted. I raised my hand to bang on the door, making good use of the huge knocker. Not knowing who might answer, I took several steps back while I rooted around in my sack, getting the package ready. I admit I was nervous, even though the criminal custom of shooting the messenger had gone mostly out of style. It was that "mostly" part that made me jumpy. Courier assassination carried a hefty fine and the heaviest of jail terms, but some people tended to act first, think later.

After a minute or two, it was clear no one was coming to answer the door so I approached once more, this time striking the door even more loudly five times. I also called "hello" for good measure. Finally, after another couple of minutes and a few more bangs on the door, the huge door swung open towards me, making me spring back. Hidden hinges that swung outwards were a safety measure that would make it even harder for the door to get battered in. The doors were over nine inches thick. Whoever lived here was definitely paranoid, whichever side of the law they lay.

"What?" a man asked, drawing my attention away from the door. He looked like he'd just woken up, eyes blinking owlishly at me from behind large glasses, white hair sticking up at all angles. His eyes took a moment to focus on me, but when they did a smile slowly creased his cheeks. "Well, hello lovely. Are you a present for dear old Otto?"

I took a moment to process what he'd implied, considered decking him but decided against it. Instead, I kept my distance, flashing the small identifying bangle I wore on my wrist. The day I'd been sworn in as a courier, I'd received one of the coveted bangles made from calressium, a metal so rare and tightly controlled by the Peoples Galactic Confederation that almost no one else had access to it. GalCon used it to identify government employees, welding the bangles on when you began your service. The only way to remove them was by cutting them off with special shears made of the same metal. The PGPS bauble ensured my access to almost anywhere I could ever want to go. It was a good system, every ounce of metal accounted for and forged with nanotech trackers, though of course, those didn't work here on Renga. It didn't matter. The government assumed anyone rich enough to procure some calressium on their own wouldn't need to forge a bracelet: they could buy their way in wherever they wanted to go. I would wear the bangle for the rest of my life, even after retirement unless I was somehow dishonored – in which case I might lose not just my bracelet but also the hand. One did not enter government service lightly.

"Otto Torriko?" I asked briskly. "I'm with the PGPS. I have a package for you."

I took a small step forward and thrust a heavy box into his hands. His smile grew even bigger as his eyes scanned the return address.

"Just in time," he murmured. He smelled the package as if it was perfumed with an aphrodisiac, sighing contentedly. He nodded, satisfied. "I've got mail that's been needing picking up. Lief!" he yelled over his shoulder into the dark interior. "Get me those letters." He turned back to me, angling his head. "Gotta say, I was wondering when you people were going to get here. You're running late."

"Special couriers don't run on a timetable, sorry," I said coolly. "If you have a problem with our service you'll have to take it up with the postmaster general." I made a show of rummaging through my pack, following procedure. "If you'd like to fill out a complaint, I have a form right here."

It would be the second complaint anyone had filed through me in over three years, but we had to carry the forms on our person, just in case. Otto peered at me over his glasses, considering.

"I'll let it slide this time. I value my privacy, as I'm sure you may have noticed. But I'm used to you people coming on a schedule. What happened to Stephor? I haven't seen him in weeks."

"Extended paternity leave. That baby of his is too cute to pass up spending time with."

"I've heard that about babies," he said slowly. "Though I can't say I've ever felt the pull myself. How about you, luv? Interested in making a few?"

It was literally the worst pickup line anyone had ever cast in my direction. And the second time he'd stepped out of line. Annoyed, the small whirlwind of dust that began to swirl around my feet rose out of habit, a warning to stay out of my space.

"Sorry, you'll have to do better than that," I laughed, watching a thin young man handed Otto a bundle of letters, the recycled cylinders incongruously tied together with a red ribbon, a bouquet of dull grays and greens reflecting their bamboo origins. The man peered at me nervously as I answered. "I'm not looking to procreate."

Otto reddened and the thin man gaped at me.

"Just as well," Otto said, eyes hardening and looking at my ears pointedly. "We don't need more of your kind around here. Next time, don't be late. Lief, tip the lady."

Otto turned on his heels and stalked away, Lief thrusting a handful of bills into my hands. Before I could say a word, explain that couriers weren't supposed to accept tips, he'd reached out and pulled the door back, slamming it shut.

Okay, I thought. *Well, that was weird.* Stefan's sector might have been more trouble than it was worth. Though when I saw the denominations of Yendars in my hand, I could see Otto and Lief wanted to make sure I'd come back. I looked at a complaint form in my other hand, thinking that I might have to fill it out myself, money aside. Sexual harassment of a courier could get you banned from the delivery maps. And the whole set-up was plain weird. But Otto hadn't done anything, not really, other than be rude. I decided to give him one more chance, then I'd see. I couldn't even be sure whether Otto was more concerned with having me overlook his crass comments or the lack of access to his fortress, but either way the money Lief had handed me would do some good at the local woman's shelter in Chalinex.

I just hoped whatever I'd handed Otto wasn't illegal.

As I hefted myself up and over yet another boulder, the process of leaving more arduous than my arrival, I made a mental note to ask Stephor about his unusual clients. Once I was safely out on the quarry, I made for a nearby stand of trees and took a moment to center myself, leaning comfortably against a large pine. Still feeling slightly defiled and agitated from my encounter with Otto, I took a cleansing sip of mint-laced water from my canteen and checked my route map.

Would all of Stephor's customers be so shady? Could this be the real reason he was extending his leave?

The next few, at least, proved relatively innocuous.

A package filled with small but valuable family mementos from a deceased great-aunt five planets away, the family of rice farmers both melancholy and overjoyed upon receiving the contents intact. They plied me with sticky rice cakes and heavily sweetened black tea before sending me on my way.

A pen-pal exchange of letters for a homeschooled girl living alone with her father on a small tilapia farm, the mother deceased three years earlier. The letters cheered her somewhat, but I kicked her smile up another notch by making the clothes dance on the line as they dried, the warm breeze I'd summoned speeding up the process.

A freshly printed prayer book for the small religious compound, twenty co-op houses centered around the central temple hall. I didn't ask what or who they worshipped, and they didn't try to convert me. I appreciated their restraint, though I suspected it had something more to do with the whispers of witchcraft I caught as I left than any godly manners. I made another mental note, this time to alert the Enso about the prejudice I was encountering out on the job. Also known as The Circle, The Enso was headquartered in Puraimura and served as the self-governing council for magic users.

As mages, we ascribed to the ideals of harmony and balance, learning that all are connected so there must be no harm. If anyone stepped out of line, it was the council's job to make sure they stepped back into formation. It was either that or risk attracting bad press from the regs. We'd heard about witch trials happening on other planets. Most of the time, there wasn't even any actual real magic involved, just superstition and fear. The Enso had been formed long ago, almost as soon as the magic had begun to appear on Renga. We policed ourselves, and the regs knew it. Gave them a sense of calm, I guess, to know that rule number one was to harm none. Like, that meant we couldn't be so bad, right?

Even if some of them did still call us demons.

I was excited to get to Chalinex city where I had several stops – the best one, of course, being my brother's workplace. I had three stops in the city to make first, and then a few more after before I could head home. As much as I wanted to push through to see Jonah, there was no way I would make it there before the middle of the night. I might as well spend the evening where I was, enjoy the wilds. I made camp once again, unrolling my small inflatable bedroll and laying down to look up the stars. I pulled out a small package of smoked fish jerky that the homeschooled girl had handed me, gnawing happily, and fell asleep to the soft music of the stars.

CHAPTER 5

no matter the rain -
names no deluge can clean foul
mean streets like corpses

The sky had opened over Chalinex City to purge the filth from the streets, but all it did was make the smell of dissolution more present. No petrichor here, only the fetid scent of rotting flesh and humanity crammed between the seams of stone like mortar. I didn't mind the rain but this was not my city. A man bumped into me, hard.

"Yokai," he spat.

I pulled my hood up over my head and glared at his back, sending the driving rain towards him, causing him to stumble.

"Pig," I whispered. Though to be fair I rather liked pigs. Bigots, not so much. Still, the encounter reminded me to take care here, stay focused and keep my head up. I was so used to the wilds and Prime, but there were so many newcomers on Renga, more every day, it seemed. All of them regs.

How long would it be before they tried to push us out? It didn't matter that this was our planet, that we'd mined it, settled it, made the atmosphere breathable, the land livable. Regs always wanted to make worlds suit them, and not the other way around. The technological advances of our species were a testament to the hubris that came with it. Sure, there were laws against ethnic cleansing, but that hadn't stopped exterminations on other planets. I was glad we had the Enso, glad my people had had the foresight to create its own circle of protection.

Chalinex had been carefully planned and built over two hundred years ago. It was supposed to be a shiny sample of what civilized living could be like on Renga. Better than Prime, a place worthy of those with more sophisticated tastes and elite fortunes.

As beautiful as it may have begun, as perfect as the architecture was, its citizens were not. Chalinex had quickly been overrun with more than its fair share of criminals – third sons of mafia families from distant solar systems looking to make their mark and make their parents proud. So many crime families, so many pissing contests. First the cops, and then The Circle tried to keep people in line, but it was a constant battle to keep the underworld from rising up and overrunning the planet.

Yet, men like the one on the street had the balls to call me the demon.

I shook my head. I didn't really understand how Jonah could live here, how he could stomach the corruption. I knew there had to be dirty cops at his station, people on the grift. I wished that it was Jonah was proud of our people, that he'd become a policeman to protect us, but I knew that wasn't the case. He resented our kind, hated being different. He could pass for human and he did every day. And I could have forgiven him for that, I already had, but he couldn't forgive me. Not for my ears, not for my magic. Not for being his twin, marking him.

Jonah liked to pretend that I didn't exist. I'd let him get away with it for the last several years because I understood why he felt the way he did. But family was family, it didn't come with conditions. The simple truth was that I missed him, though I couldn't really have told you why. Would I have felt the same if we hadn't been twins, shared a womb? I didn't know. But we had.

Which is why I found myself standing in front of the precinct, rain pouring down around me, nerves warring with excitement. For far too long, I watched people come and go, the traffic heavy through the doors. Finally, I steeled myself and moved to the side, taking a moment to compose myself in an alcove. My shadowy reflection was barely readable in the dark polished marble of the wall, but I could see enough to tell I looked like a drowned kitten. I breathed slowly out my mouth, in through my nose, a circular breath with no end and no beginning. The energy built within me and then I watched the water lift from my cloak and hair like a thousand shining diamonds suspended momentarily in the air before they fell to the ground. I fluffed up my hair one last time, then stalked towards the entrance, to where my brother waited unawares like a drowsy panther.

Inside, the burly cop at the front desk ground out one word as if it cost him maximum effort.

"Business?"

"PGPS," I answered just as curtly. I held up my wrist showing the official bangle welded there, the metal giving off its signature teal shine. The cop eyed bracelet. As a local law enforcement officer, he did not have one of his own, only a simple brass badge.

"Post runner, huh? Leave the mail here, I'll sign for it."

"No can do. Package requires Recipient Receipt." I checked the package again. "It's for Detective Lyric Pearce. Also, I was wondering if Jonah Kozan was around?"

"Kozan?" he asked as he picked up the phone. "What do you want him for?"

"That's private, sorry. Just tell him Nikta's here."

The cop looked intrigued, his eyes straying to my ears. Probably thinking I was one of Jonah's girlfriends. "I'll let him know you're here, though you might have to wait a spell. He's got his hands full with some kid he brought in tripping on the feed."

"The feed?" I asked, but the cop held up a hand, speaking into the phone.

"Yeah, Pearce, you've got a package here, Recipient Receipt. No, how would I know what it is? It's a package, plain brown paper. Sender?" The cop looked at me and I shrugged. "Don't know. Look, you gonna come sign for this thing or what? Yeah, okay."

The cop huffed with exasperation and hung up the phone. "He'll be out in a minute. Guy's a real pain in the you-know-what if you ask me. Like I ain't got nothing better to do than play secretary."

As if to prove his point, an elderly woman came in dragging a young woman by the ear. Instantly, she started yelling at the desk cop, complaining that her niece had stolen her best pair of earrings and she wanted to press charges. The young woman, pointed to her ear where it had turned bright red and wailed, asking how she could possibly have stolen them when she didn't even have pierced ears. Rolling his eyes at me, the cop leaned handed the aunt a form to fill out and instructed her to release the young lady. Immediately, the niece demanded a form of her own, which started an entirely fresh bout of yelling and whining.

Bemused, I moved out of the way and stood near the inner doors to watch the telenovela unfolding before me. A man near my own age, maybe a few years older, came out and stood next to me, cocking his head as he listened to the drama. I glanced up at him, taking in hard chiseled features that contrasted with warm honeyed skin and an amused gleam in his eye. He was dressed as a civilian, no doubt just wrapping up his own police business. Handsome and a bit dangerous-looking.

"Friends of yours?" he asked, barely looking at me.

"Definitely not."

He nodded, looking preoccupied, and seemed to rouse himself. "Right. Well, that's enough fun for the day. Duty calls." He strode away without another word and checked in at the desk, his movements efficient and spare. I couldn't hear what was said over the din of the two woman and the three cops who had arrived to try and handle the situation, but I did notice the desk jockey pointing a figure over in my direction.

Ah. So this was the detective.

The man came back looking cross, irritation icing his pale green eyes.

"Why didn't you say you had a package for me?"

"Why didn't you ask?" I retorted.

"I have things I should be doing, important cases I'm working on. I don't need some post jockey messing around and cutting into my time."

"Excuse you? How about this – I have important packages to deliver, people who are depending on me. I don't need some self-important cop-"

"Detective."

"Detective, fine, wasting my time, either. Name?"

"Lyric Pearce. You have my package?"

"Maybe. You have ID?" I wasn't always so careful about following procedure by the letter, but this guy was getting on my last nerves. I raised my eyebrows

47

and waited for him to fish his badge out of his pocket. He shoved the metal pin at me and I shook my head.

"Nuh-uh, sorry." I handed it back. "I'm going to need something with your picture on it."

Muttering under his breath, he pulled out his wallet and dug out a confederally-issued Galactic ID. I thought I might have picked up something about kittens needing a special kind of lockup, but I decided not to listen too closely. Even if I did have the kind of hearing that made it nearly impossible.

Acting like I had all the time in the world, I let my eyes roam over his ID, memorizing his address, blood type and age. I'd been right – he was three years my senior. Finally, I handed it back, along with the Recipient Receipt and a pen.

"Print your name and sign here, along with your ID number. Perfect, thanks. Here's your package. Would you mind sending Jonah Kozan out when you go back in? I have something for him as well." Somehow, the idea of revealing anything of myself to this pompous ass was repellant.

"Fine." He went back through the heavy swinging doors without another word, not even a thank you. Ingrate. I was glad I hadn't revealed my identity to him. A man like that didn't deserve to know my name.

CHAPTER 6

family is family
not seeing is a flower

Despite his rude manner, Detective Pearce seemed to have followed through. Jonah shouldered his way through the doors not two minutes later looking harassed.

"Nikta," he said, shoving his hands into the pockets of his grey police uniform. "What are you doing here?"

"What, can't a girl say hello?" I said lightly, the words tasting bitter on my tongue. "I had business here. New route, a package for Detective Pearce."

His face, so much like mine, a bit broader across the cheeks, a bit lighter in the eye, turned sour. "Yeah, you managed to piss him off somehow. If you've spoiled my shot at making detective, I'll-"

"Never speak to me again? You're doing pretty well on that already. Relax, little brother, I didn't tell him who I was."

Jonah narrowed his eyes at me, and grabbed my arm, steering me through the doors into the bowels of the station. And when I say bowels, I mean it. The place was grimy, the floors covered with dirt. Whatever I'd thought of the chaos outside in the waiting area, it was ten times worse in here. It seemed like everywhere you turned, someone was spewing hate at someone else, complaining, whining or yelling.

"How can you work here?" I asked, shocked. Jonah had loved camping with Jiji as much as me. I didn't understand how he could bear working in this stewpot of venality.

He shrugged, sinking into his seat at a desk in a dark corner. "Ten people, ten colors. The law makes everyone equal. I care about this planet just as much as you do. I don't want to see it go to hell."

"Equal, really? Then why don't you want people to know who you really are?" I asked, leaning forward and watching him flinch. "How can you talk about diversity if you can't even admit your own heritage?"

"Look, I know what you think of me. I'm sorry if you think I'm not living up to my potential just because I don't walk around introducing myself as a nekokai, but I'm a little busy here trying to clean up the city."

This time, it was my turn to flinch. "How can you use that word?" Nekokai was the most terrible thing you could call the chimeras on Renga, a slur deriving from trickster legends of ancient feline Yokai demons, the Nekomato and Bakemato. It literally meant "faulty feline" or "strange cat," as if our genetic modifications or magics made us deformed, inhuman.

"It's just a word," he sighed, straightening the papers on his desk, not looking me in the eye.

"And words have power. You know that as well as I do. What would mother say?"

"I don't know. She's not here, is she, so it hardly matters." His tone was sullen as he folded his arms across his chest. His words went through me like an arrow to my heart.

"You can't mean that."

"Can't I?"

"Fine," I said, straightening. "But what about me? I'm here, dammit. We're family. Don't you miss that?"

"Sometimes," he admitted. "But you know what they say. Not seeing is a flower."

"Seriously? You'd rather imagine how great I'm doing than actually see it with your own two eyes? It hurt when you left, when Mama died and you left me and Jiji all alone, but I thought you'd at least keep in touch."

"Yeah? Well, it hurts to see you," he snapped. "Why can't you leave me alone? I'm happy here. People think I'm a reg, and I can forget what happened in school. I can feel normal. Not like some freak."

I reeled back in my chair, my face on fire. He might as well have slapped me. His powers had lashed out with his words, stinging my skin with heat.

"Shit, Nikta, I'm sorry, I didn't mean-"

"To use your powers on me like some freak?" I hissed. "I told you words have power. Your magic is unstable, you obviously haven't been practicing. It has no outlet."

I said this quietly as I pulled my hood up over my hair, shadowing my face so that his compatriots wouldn't see what he'd done, the blisters rising on my skin.

"Stop. I'm sorry. Let me help." He placed his hands on my cheeks, drawing the fire out, cooling the skin. We'd always been able to heal each other, our special gemini gift. It had been useful, a regular necessity growing up around each other, bickering as siblings do. Even before the Olympic scouts had come and gone, Jonah had been restless, hard to please. I had always been the softer of us, truly at peace with who I was. Older by ten minutes than Jonah, smaller by five inches, but strong as calressium according to Mama.

If I was so strong, why did Jonah make me want to burrow into my cloak and cry? Determined not to show him how much he'd hurt me, I sat up straighter and pushed my hood back.

"Thanks. I guess I'll get going then." I stood up, placing a hand on the back of my chair so he couldn't see it shaking. "Packages to deliver, you know the drill."

He looked up at me, regret etched across his face. "Yeah, I do. I'll call, okay?"

"Sure you will. You going to give your sister a hug or what?"

He looked around the station nervously, obviously gauging what people would think if they saw him embracing one of my kind. Our kind, no matter how he might look on the outside. I rolled my eyes. "Never mind. I'll see myself out."

"Nikta," he said, shifting uncomfortably in his seat. But he didn't rise.

I took a step back, raised a hand to head off any platitudes.

"Don't bother, broth-"

And then I was soaring through the air, colliding with my brother, thunder in my ears.

CHAPTER 7

wind undermines trust
healing only goes so deep
arrested by song

My ears stung as if hornets had taken to nesting within the sensitive folds. I lay on Jonah in a heap, our legs tangled together on the floor where his chair had toppled backwards. His eyes were closed, a drop of blood at the corner his mouth. He'd clearly hit his head hard on the floor. Hopefully, he still had all his teeth. His tongue, well... Maybe our relationship would fare better if he couldn't speak.

I considered leaving him as he lay, but of course I couldn't. I placed one of my own hands on his face, groaning at the pain the slight movement caused. My spine felt like it had been rammed with a calressium girder. For all I knew, it had. What the hell had happened? Even as I worked to merge my energy with Jonah's and heal our wounds, I craned my neck to take stock of the devastation around us. A directional blast had torn through the wall behind us, leaving a narrow wake of dust and destruction behind. All around me, people were slowly climbing to their feet from where they'd taken cover, taking stock.

Jonah stirred and I scrambled off him. He could finish healing the normal way, nice and slow like the regs he envied so much. I watched as one of his fellow cops rushed over to help him sit up.

"You okay, Jones?" The woman looked at him with more than the usual dose of concern and I saw Jonah's eyes flick to mine and back to hers before he answered.

"Yeah, I'm okay, I think. What happened?"

"Not sure," she said, shaking her head. "What about you, ma'am? You okay?"

"Me, oh sure. I'm light on my feet. Plus, this big oaf here broke my fall. I'll leave you to it, then." I held up my wrist, brandishing my identifier. "Places to be, mail to deliver."

Jonah nodded, looking relieved. Whoever this woman was to him, she clearly didn't know everything about him. "Ohalo," he said, using the word that wrapped thanks, blessings and godspeed all in one.

I nodded, not quite able to speak, and turned, drawing my hood up again. I was almost to the door when a hand clamped roughly on my shoulder.

"Not so fast," a man snarled, yanking me back. I whirled, my eyes meeting those of Lyric Pearce. "You're coming with me."

"What? Why?" I asked, trying to pull away.

"Because that package you just delivered almost killed me, that's why. Surprised to see me still breathing?"

"Me? No, of course not, I- Wait. My package did this?" The blood drained from my face.

"So you admit it then," he sneered, dragging me across the station through the chaos.

"Admit what? I didn't mean it was actually my package, of course it was yours. "

"Right. A mysterious package with no return address explodes and you have nothing to do with it. Sure." He shoved me roughly into a chair in the holding cell we'd entered. "What's your game, runner? If you even are a runner at all. Who paid you to carry that package?"

"No one paid me," I scoffed. "I'm an employee for the PGPS. I don't need to take side jobs."

"So, what then? You work with a political group? A crime ring? Who sent you?"

I sighed, trying to stay calm. "No one sent me. I work for the PGPS," I repeated. "Your package was marked Carry with Care, which means it gets delivered by post runner. It came through the Prime sorting office, where I picked it up a few days ago." My brow furrowed. "So, I was carrying a bomb on me all that time? Florence is gonna be so pissed."

"Florence, who is that?"

"My supervisor."

Pearce snorted, looking unconvinced.

"No, really. And she is gonna be furious. Our sniffers are supposed to pick up any illegal contents before they head out. Something like that," I waved my hands towards the blast area beyond the walls, "that isn't supposed to be allowed to happen."

The detective eyed me suspiciously. "Exactly why I'm not inclined to believe your little act. So tell me, why are you here? Who sent you."

I growled a bit, clenching my hands into fists. *Hold it together, Nikta*, I told myself. *Assaulting a law officer is a criminal offense.* "I already told you, I'm just a runner."

"A runner with a bit of a temper, it seems," he said, raising an eyebrow to the small breeze that had started swirling through the room, ruffling his hair. "Do I need to remind you to control your magic?"

"I don't know. Do I need to remind you that it's illegal to hold me without a charge?"

"Actually, I can hold you for twenty-six hours without access to counsel or booking you on charges. That's what happens to suspected terrorists, or did you forget to brush up on the law before you decided to assault an officer?"

"Oh, come on. I had nothing to do with that!"

His hands slammed down on the table and he leaned down in my face, his cheeks turning red with anger. "I will be the judge of that!"

And I swear I didn't mean to do it, but the way he'd gotten in my face like that, it triggered a stress response and well… that small wind I'd been nurturing slapped him back several feet. Now, it was my own turn to blush, but not with anger.

Shame.

"I'm sorry, I didn't mean to-"

His eyes shuttered, the light going out of them.

"You just bought yourself a night in lockup with that little trick of yours, Miss-"

"Kozan. Nikta Kozan."

For a moment, he looked confused. "Kozan? Didn't you ask for-"

"Yes. Jonah is my brother," I admitted, massaging a building ache in my forehead with one hand. Jonah was going to kill me. "And as much as he can't stand me, I'm pretty sure he'll tell you that there's no way I had anything to do with that package."

Pearce narrowed his eyes at me. "Cops have been betrayed by family before. It wouldn't be the first time."

"Look, this isn't going anywhere. Either get Jonah in here to vouch for me or put me in lockup. I'm not going to sit here and be antagonized by you for something I didn't do." I crossed my arms over my chest and stared up at him defiantly. Inside, though, I was quaking. I had assaulted an officer. It had been an accident, excusable perhaps after being shaken in the blast, but still – The

Enso wouldn't look kindly on it, never mind the law. Lockup would be kind compared to some of the punishments the Enso were known to mete out. "In fact," I said, angling my chin at him, "maybe I should be the one threatening you with legal action. That package of yours sent me flying across the room, knocked me to the floor. Maybe I hurt myself. Hmm. Yeah. I think my knee is damaged. Oh no, what if I can't run anymore? Yeah, I think you better call my council at the PGPS."

He laughed, a cynical sound. "I don't think so. I know how strong your kind are. I doubt you even caught a bruise."

"My kind?" The hair on the back of my neck rose and the wind began to swirl again.

"Don't get your hackles up," he said, eyeing me. "You don't want to rack up more booking charges. So, is that your angle? You part of some magical anarchist group? Because I can tell you going after the police isn't going to win you any admirers. We're on your side as much as The Circle. We just want to keep the peace." He sounded conciliatory, his tone easy. If I'd had something to confess, I might have bought his act and spilled my guts, but as it was I had nothing to say.

"My kind," I ground out, "is peaceable. I will only say this one more time: I didn't do anything wrong. I don't know who tried to kill you. As annoying and rude as you are, I promise I have no desire to see you dead. In fact, I have no desire to see you at all."

He stared at me like I was a crossword that might fill itself in. Finally, he sighed.

"Are you aware that you killed my assistant, Ms. Kozan? Do you even care?"

I gasped, shocked. "Someone died?"

"You mean, someone besides your target? Yes. Duffy opens all my mail, keeps track of all my business. And now he's dead for it. That blast took off half his face. Are you proud of yourself? Still want to play innocent?"

I stared at him, pain in my chest. I couldn't breathe. I couldn't think. Someone had died?

I started to hyperventilate, thinking how close Jonah and I had come to death. For the millionth time, I wondered how he could work here.

"Look," Pearce said, watching me freak out like a bug under a glass. "If what you say is true, if the mail is all screened before you pick it up, then how is it that mine happened to have a bomb in it? You do realize, don't you, that your story makes you look even more guilty."

I tried to steady my breath, but it hurt, like razors were cutting into my lungs. And like the pain, the realization cut through me. He was right. How did his package ever make it into my hands?

And then it hit me. Our best sniffer had been running security at the back door the night I'd come through, instead of scanning packages. I spoke up, the words tumbling out of me even as the thoughts came together.

"Berman, our security guard, she had food poisoning. Joe was manning her station – he's our best sniffer. We've had a lot of people calling out lately. Our two newest recruits both just dropped out this week. I'm not even supposed to have this route, but Stephor decided to extend his paternity leave and a few of us had to split up his delivery sector, pick up his slack and add it to our own."

"Okay, so what you're telling me is that you're not even supposed to have this post? Again, you're not making yourself look any less guilty here."

"Maybe not, but don't you see? Maybe someone set it up so Berman would be sick, so that Joe would be on security. Maybe someone did something to scare those new recruits."

"That's a lot of maybes."

"It is. But that's your job, isn't it? To chase every lead?"

"What do you think I'm doing right now? A dog doesn't drop a good bone just to go off sniffing after some weak broth."

"He does if the bone tastes like crap," I shot back, my voice cracking. Some of the dust from the explosion must have gotten in there, and I was finding it harder and harder to breathe, every inhalation burning. "Look, I know what it looks like but I'm not your guy. If I was in on it, don't you think I would have done a better job? I'm not an idiot. If I wanted to kill you, I wouldn't need a bomb to do it. And your friend wouldn't be…" I trailed off, not wanting to say it.

"Dead?"

Yep, that was the word I hadn't wanted to say.

"Right, that. Look, I'm sorry, okay? I knew what I signed up for when I became a runner, but bombs? That's not supposed to be one of the dangers. Bandits, sure. Lightning storms and predatory animals in the forest, okay. Those things I can handle. But bombs? No."

Pearce pulled out the chair across from me and sat down, leaning back as if he was completely relaxed, like we were just two pals, hanging out.

"Okay. Let's say that I was feeling inclined to believe you. I get what you're saying. I myself signed up for a job with danger in the description and unfortunately, bombs sometimes do come along with that work."

"Right then. You have heard the saying, 'don't shoot the messenger'? This isn't my fault."

Pearce slid me a skeptical look. "My uncle worked as a carrier. Not a post runner, just a regular driver for the delivery trucks. I know how hard it is to sneak munitions through the mail. What you're saying, even you have to admit it doesn't wash. Are you saying someone orchestrated to get your best sniffer off the line, and someone less skilled or possibly even involved let the package through?"

"I don't know," I said, throwing up my hands. "What if it was concealed with magic? Maybe the package was shielded?

He shook his head. "Again, it doesn't wash. Your sniffers are supposed to be able to detect that."

"But maybe-"

He held up a hand, interrupting me. "We're not getting anywhere. I don't know if I can believe you, and I'm not inclined to let a suspected terrorist go. I'm going to keep you here." I opened my mouth to protest but he continued. "Look, I'm keeping you here for now. I'm going to check with your supervisor. If everything you're telling me checks out, well, then it might actually be safer for you to stay here for a while. If you're not part of the scheme, maybe you were intended to be the scapegoat. Do you have any enemies that you know of? At work? Or maybe old clients?"

"What? No. Everybody likes me." He eyed me dubiously. "They do," I insisted.

"Well, then maybe you were supposed to make it out. After all, unless the person knew your brother was here, who could have expected you to stick around?" Pearce stood and looked down at me. "I'm going to go make some calls."

"And what am I supposed to do? I have a route to run and-"

"And you better hope your story checks out." I tried to make a face at him. Instead, I was caught up in a fit of choking, each cough feeling like it was pushing the dust deeper into my throat.

"Detective," I choked out as he put his hand on the door.

"What?"

"Can I get a glass of water? My throat, I think the explosion... well..."

My words died under his blank stare and I shifted my eyes to his fingers, strong yet fine, holding the door. A plain gold band adorned one finger. Someone out there loved this man and today they'd almost lost him.

"Yeah, fine. Water. But nothing else, I'm not your waitress."

"Yeah," I retorted. "And I'm not your murderer."

Scowling, he nodded, the door slamming shut behind him.

CHAPTER 8

one life, one encounter – fate
baits a hook with redemption

I was deep in thought wondering how long I was going to be stuck there when the door was flung open, banging against the wall. If I'd been any kind of a real cat, I would have arched my back and jumped back, hissing. But I was more human than anything else, and so I just raised one eyebrow. Expecting Detective Pearce, I was slightly relieved to see Jonah stalk purposefully across the room and plunk a dingy glass of water in front of me. He stood there, out of reach with his arms folded across his chest, watching as I sucked the water down. Like everything else in Chalinex, it carried an acrid, soulless flavor. The liquid was cool, though, and felt like an icy balm to the irritated lining of my throat. When it was all gone, I looked gratefully up at my brother.

"Thanks, Jonah."

"Thanks. Thanks? Is that all you have to say to me?"

"What do you want me to say?"

"Do you know what's going on out there right now?"

"Not really." I waved a hand at my surroundings. "Not much of view in here. Why don't you tell me?"

"Duffy Merritt is dead, for one. A confirmed hit that Pearce ready to pin on your head. He's been trying to crack this new magical drug ring, and here you are, delivering death packages."

"Jonah, it's not my fault. You know I wouldn't-"

He cut me off. "Look, of course I know you didn't have anything to do with it. But someone set you up as a perfect patsy to take the fall. And now everybody is going to know who I am. What I am. Do you have any idea how fast the gossip spreads around a police station? They're like little kids out there."

"Again, not my fault. I'm sorry that your cover is blown, that now everybody knows that you have a magical yokai sister, but maybe hiding who you are wasn't the best idea to begin with."

"What would you know about it?" he asked, sour.

"I know you," I said softly. "You can't erase your heritage. It's who you are."

"I was doing fine until you showed up. You just had to come, didn't you, Nikta?" He paused, his expression bitter, but I stayed silent. When Jonah got like this, it was useless to argue with him. He'd only become angrier, more unreasonable. We held each other's gaze for several more beats, and then he sighed, visibly coming down a rung from his ladder to ire. "Just don't tell anyone we're twins, okay?"

"Don't you think that Pearce is going to put it all together? We have the same birthday, it's not exactly hard to figure out."

"Promise me," he repeated.

"Whatever. You can go on pretending you're a reg, that you don't have any powers or anything, that you're an apple that grew from an entirely different tree if you want. But if you ask me, anyone who would think less of you for being a settler isn't worth the air they're breathing."

"That's not how it is."

"No? Tell me, Jonah. Is everyone here a bigot or is it just you and Pearce?

"I'm not a bigot," he insisted, though the guilty look in his eye made it clear he knew what a fine line he was walking. "Being a cop means you have to gain the trust of everyone and fact is, a lot of the newer regs don't trust our kind. They worry about how powerful we could be if we-"

"You know what, Jonah?" I interrupted him. "The hard fact is that we used to be the majority on Renga and we had a chance to rule it. But we didn't do anything out of the ordinary. We didn't create some magical monarchy or kill off regs when they started coming. We followed galactic rules. We did everything a normal person would do and when the normal people arrived here in droves we didn't freak out. We went out of our way to make them feel welcome. We formed the Enso so they would feel safer, so they could know we aimed to keep our own kind in check. So don't you start quoting that reg bull at me. You want to apologize for what you are, start with what's in your heart, not your DNA. Don't you dare try and make me feel sorry for what I am. I'm a person, just like you. Just like Jiji, and Mama. And I'll be damned if I'm going to feel bad about any of it."

Jonah's spine softened and he smoothed his long fingers over his eyebrows, massaging his temples as he grimaced. "I know, I know. I'm sorry. It's just been hard, okay. You breeze through every situation so easily, but for me everything's been a struggle."

"Not everything, Jonah," I murmured. "You were happy. We were happy. You had a good childhood. So, you couldn't go to the Olympics. You've had a good life."

He slammed his hands down on the table. "I lost everything that day. Every hope I ever had was crushed in one moment."

"But Jonah, you knew it would happen. You knew the rules."

"It was my life. It was all I ever wanted."

"I know. But there are other ways you could have continued with your swimming, you didn't have to-"

"Enough. I can't talk about this with you anymore."

"Is that why you left? Because you didn't want to talk to me? Do you know how hard it was for me after you left? It was like the bottom dropped out. Mom died, and then Jiji... I took care of them, sat with them as they died, all by myself while you were licking your wounds or whatever."

"I know, I'm sorry. I feel bad about that."

"Do you?"

He looked away, unable to meet my eyes. "Of course, I do. It's part of why I haven't been home."

"Seriously, little brother? You think you can make up for not being around by not being around? What is wrong with you?"

"You're so grown up. You tell me. I'm sure you have a list written up somewhere, maybe a haiku?" he spat.

I froze, shocked by the vicious tone of his voice. "I-"

I'm not sure what I would have said, if it would have been civil or heartfelt or as dead on the inside as I felt just then. I didn't have to finish, because Detective Pearce came back with a handful of papers and a dull brown cylinder.

"Okay, so far your story's checking out. I still have a couple of people that need to return my call. In the meantime, I have another question for you."

"Okay," I said, sitting up taller in my seat, a little nervous. I glanced at Jonah and Pearce followed my gaze.

"Jonah, don't you have a report you need to finish filing? Can you give us a minute?"

My brother looked surprised, and for a moment I imagined that he might insist on staying. Looking out for my rights, my welfare. Then he ducked his head.

"Yes. Yes, sir. I do." He slipped quickly out of the room. Pearce pulled out the chair across from me.

"Right, here's the deal. I'm still waiting to hear back from some people but I'm beginning to believe that you're on the up and up. In fact, I'm pretty damn sure of it," he admitted.

"So, can I go?"

"No. I have protocol to follow. After talking to my own sources in Prime, I'm inclined to believe you, like I said. But you're in a unique position, whether you're involved in or not. As a courier, you can get in places we can't. And you're not exactly a defenseless civilian. I talked to your supervisor, Florence, and she agreed to let you work undercover for me."

"Undercover?" I said, leaning way back in my seat. Anything to get away from the crazy man across from me. "Do I look stupid to you? Only an idiot would want to get involved with whatever is going on here. I mean somebody's trying to blow you up. Not exactly on my bucket list, if you know what I mean."

"Be that as it may," he said drily, "I'm going to need you to do something for me. Deliver this letter." He picked up the tube and I readied myself to protest. His mouth tightened. "If you're not willing to do it, then I can call somebody in right now to lock you up for the night." Rancor vibrated through his voice, sharp yet smoky like whisky.

"Florence would never have agreed to this, I don't believe you."

"She agreed quickly, once I reminded her that it was her facility that had let the bomb through in the first place. Do I need to remind you, too?"

"No," I muttered, scribbling idly on the back of some of the papers in front of me.

Pearce didn't say anything, but I could feel his gaze on me. Weighing me down, heavier than calressium. Finally, I looked up.

"What?"

"Are you aware that you are drawing on official police documents?" he asked. "What is that, anyway-"

"Nothing," I said, coloring. "Sorry." I started to erase the marks.

He pulled the paper away from me. "Are these characters? Dare I hope, a confession?"

I snorted. "You should be so lucky. No, not a confession. Just a poem," I admitted.

"A poem?"

"Haiku," I clarified. "Nervous habit."

He squinted at the words, lips moving. "A life, a meeting? My hiragana's not too good. Been trying to learn since I came here, but..."

"You're close," I admitted. "One life, one encounter. It's an old saying, basically about how one moment can change your whole life."

"Ah," he said, looking at me differently now. "And the rest?"

"Ask your hiragana teacher," I said flippantly, not entirely comfortable with the sudden interest in his eyes. Interest that seemed more to do with me as a woman than as a person of interest. Jonah was pissed enough at me as it was, I wasn't going to sleep where he ate, too.

"Fine," he said, his expression shuttering. He flipped the paper back over, shoved it towards me, tapping on a woman's picture. "This woman, she died last week of a heart attack, brought on by starvation and malnutrition. These reports, here? More deaths. Ostensibly, each died of natural causes, but the vics' families and friends all say the same thing."

"Which is?" I asked.

"See for yourself." He shrugged, standing up and pacing the room when I started flipping through the pile.

"Victim believed addicted to the feed? What's that?"

"A new magical drug, according to whispers on the streets. You haven't heard of it?"

I shook my head. "I stay away from synthetic highs, always have."

"Well, it's hitting the streets of Chalinex pretty hard. These days if you don't know someone using the feed, then you don't know no one."

I quirked an eyebrow at him. "Are you implying that I have no friends?"

"Not implying. Just saying. Rumors started popping up three months ago, but the deaths, those are new. My best guess is the deaths are the first users, the ones who've been feeding the longest. We can't confirm anything though, since we haven't been able to get our hands on a sample of the drug. All we know is that the drops seem to be arranged through the mail."

"And you say it's a magical drug? Have you contacted the Circle about this?" I said, waving a hand over the files.

"Not yet."

"But why not? They need to know-" He watched me, his gaze cool like cucumbers and iced sake. And it hit me. "You think they might be involved. That they did this." I stood, rising to his level. We glared at each other across the room.

"Easy now. Don't give me another reason to arrest you," he warned.

"Arrest me? You idiot! You have a magical problem and you haven't called in the Enso? We take care of our own. Police our own. You're not equipped to handle this."

"You don't know me. You don't know what I'm capable of." He spoke lightly, but I heard the steel underneath, wondered where he'd come from, what he'd done before coming to Renga.

"Well, I know you're not bomb-proof," I scoffed.

"Please, Ms. Kozan. Do yourself a favor and don't make any jokes about bombs. Have a seat, and I'll tell you what I need from you. Agree, and you can be on your way."

Resigned, I plopped back into my seat. "Fine. What's in this letter you want me to carry?"

"We think it's a drop setup. A suspected dealer ditched it when he saw our people following him. It's not another bomb, if that's what you're worried about. It's been sniffed."

"I should hope so. You really don't know what's in it?"

"You carried an explosive device all the way here. You didn't know that was in it, or so you say."

I rolled my eyes. "I didn't."

"Then you can carry this without knowing anything more."

"But that package went through proper channels. This doesn't even have a postmark."

"It's got postage on it," he said mildly, tapping the paper.

"But no postmark. No return address. It doesn't say where it originated from. Anyone with half a brain would see it's not legit."

"Fine," he said, reaching in his pocket and pulling out a red pen. "Why don't you draw me one."

"It doesn't work that way. It's not done by hand. You need a stamp and-"

"So, I'll get somebody to put an authentic looking postmark on it. Then will you carry the package?"

I hesitated.

"Or do you prefer jail time?"

"I'll carry it. So long as I'm not under arrest?"

"For now."

"Do we sign something? Do I get a guarantee?"

"Honey, nothing in this life is guaranteed." His gaze softened a bit. "This shouldn't put you in any danger. We'll get it stamped. You'll be fine. And you'll be helping us save lives."

"And it's not like you're giving me any other options," I whispered weighing the package in my hands. I looked up. "Are you?"

"No," he admitted. "I'm not."

"Then I'll do it." I tossed the mail back at him. "Get a proper postmark on it and I'll carry your damn letter. I don't suppose this place is on my route?"

"It's not too far from here. Besides, Florence knows what you're up to and you don't run on a strict timetable, right?"

"No, I don't," I said, annoyed that he actually knew something about how special couriers ran. "Why do I feel like I'm going to regret this?"

"Can't say. Just don't make me regret giving you a chance to prove yourself. Deliver the letter, make your way back here. That's all." Pearce stood, left the room letter in hand.

And left me wondering what I'd agreed to.

CHAPTER 9

freedom feels easy
till money's eyes scrutinize:
mail masks a spy's task

Though it felt like I had been in the station for days, it was only early afternoon when Pearce let me go. I'd looked hard at the counterfeit stamp on the cylinder, trying to catch a flaw, but eventually I'd had to admit the station's sketch artist had done an impeccable job copying the stamp from an older piece of mail. It looked perfect.

Jonah barely looked at me when I stopped at his side to say goodbye, scarcely deigning to give me a terse nod while he pored over the paperwork covering his desk.

"Okay, see you," he said after I had explained I was to drop off the letter and return before the end of the day.

"Bye, Jonah," I said quietly and walked away.

Behind me, I heard him sigh. "Nikta, wait. Be careful out there, okay?" I turned and saw him look around. No one was listening. No one cared about a mundane exchange between a beat cop and a new informant. Because most people probably still didn't know I was his sister. How would things change for him once they did? Jonah chewed his lip, went on. "It's not like Prime City here. People have to look out for themselves here. Make sure you do the same."

Some unnamed feeling welled up in me and I couldn't quite speak. Instead, I saluted him with a grin, ducked my head and rushed out of the building. I wouldn't cry. I wouldn't.

Even if it was the first time my brother had showed concern for me in years.

I looked down at the cylinder in my hands, noted the address and stuffed it into my pack. I pulled out my sector map, compared the address to the others marked out in Chalinex city and considered. I'd already hit three locations, which left two more within city bounds. I could drop off the letter and I'd still have time to make the deliveries before I needed to head back to the station.

Pearce had warned me the address was in an upscale neighborhood, that the addressee might even be one the people bankrolling the drug. Nestra Laroche had no powers of her own, he'd assured me, but I knew who she was. She was one of those power-hungry rich kids who'd come to Renga hoping to create a fiefdom. Even in Puraimura, we'd heard about her wild week-long parties; the way she'd been buying up certain neighborhoods, bankrolling nightclubs. The rumblings that she often paid less for these things than they should have been worth. The papers speculated that her charm and beauty were wooing the opposition, that men were simply hoping to gain her good graces, perhaps secure a betrothal. Some whispered darker suspicions: that she used information as a weapon, that she blackmailed people to get what she wanted. More than one person had left Renga after they'd concluded business with Nestra Laroche, though whether it was by choice or not, no one really knew.

And now a drug dealer was mailing her a letter. How was she involved? Was she behind it all? This was what Lyric Pearce wanted to know. What he was using me to find out.

The rain, at least, had stopped. Water still dripped here and there, but for the most part the city had dried out, courtesy of the city's excellent sewer system. That, at least, was something the planners had gotten right. And, I realized as I jogged lightly along the sidewalks, some parts of Chalinex were more sightly than others. Even beautiful. My brother appeared to work in one of the seedier districts of town. The further I got from it, the nicer the homes became. Corner marketplaces became open-air food stalls; postage sized empty lots with broken swings morphed into neatly manicured parks with playgrounds; apartment complexes gave way to charming duplexes with fenced-in yards.

It was at one of these that I stopped to drop off a thick package, ringing the bell at a locked gate. The fencing was trellised with purple passionflowers, their anemone-like centers waving at me in the breeze. In the yard, children's toys had been left out: a ball, a cart, some lettered blocks. The latter, I knew, shouldn't have been left out in the rain. The door opened and a young boy ran out, probably about eight years old, while a tired-looking woman held a baby on her hip in the door.

"Delivery for Angel Oakley?" I called out, holding up the mail tube.

"That's me," she nodded. "Charlie, it's alright. You can sign for it."

Carefully, the young child printed out his full name in my book. "Perfect, thank you, Charlie," I said. Then I leaned down. "Oh, and Charlie, you might want to pick up your toys before your mother sees they're all wet."

Eyes wide, he looked at the blocks on the grass. "I will," he whispered and then ran back towards his mother. "Thank you!" he called over his shoulder.

He thrust the package at his mother. Absently, she waved to me and disappeared inside. Charlie waited a few moments and then quietly slipped back out, quickly scooping up the blocks in his arms and running back inside the house with them, kicking the ball into the bushes by the stairs as he went.

I laughed and continued on. I was glad to see that some things in Chalinex remained unspoiled.

That was before I entered the neighborhood of Nestra Laroche. Crossing a small river, I found myself among quiet streets. Gone were the charming duplexes. In their place stood vast mansions. I saw no community parks, no markets, no hint of community or commerce. Only private estates with rolling lawns, extensive gardens, ponds and fountains no doubt fed by the same aquifer as the river I'd crossed minutes before. Here stood the homes of the robber barons, the business mavens of Chalinex, the rich who had come to Renga looking to make their mark. Each house sought to stand out, to out-do its neighbor in pomp and bling. Here, there was no attempt to assimilate, to fit in, to build a community. No. Everyone here wanted to rule, and they wanted their neighbors to know it.

It should have been beautiful. I knew many people would have been impressed by the homes I jogged past. But the whole thing left a sour taste in my mouth, no sweetness like Angel. Like Charlie.

The domicile of Nestra Laroche was more castle than home. Unlike most of her neighbors, though, she had no gates. And why should she, I wondered, as I gaped at the moat circling the palatial grounds. Coming to a bridge flanked by two guards, I brandished my bangle.

"PGPS. I have a special delivery for Nestra Laroche."

"She's expecting you. Clive will see you in," the burlier of the two said, nodding for her wiry companion to lead me across the grounds. I noted two guns on Clive's hips and wondered at the tight security. It appeared Nestra had her fair share of enemies, or at least she believed she did.

"Bet you're not used to seeing places like this," Clive leered at me as we walked between two marble fountains, each with a bevy of Roman-style fawns dancing around a gorgeous reclining goddess. The marble had been polished to a mirror-like finish so that it shimmered in the starry light, the water reflecting the sky above.

I had pushed my hood back some but kept my ears covered. If this woman was indeed some kind of a criminal mastermind, the last thing I wanted was for her to try and turn me for profit. Chimeras were hot on the black market in every solar system, especially magicals.

"Can't say I have," I agreed easily, taking in the perfectly groomed topiaries along the path. "Your mistress has a fine eye."

"She does, indeed," he said proudly. I stifled a smile as I considered the fact that her eye did not extend to her help. I wasn't sure what one had to do to qualify for her employ, but handsomeness wasn't on the list, judging by Clive. Nor was intelligence. At least, not the regular kind. Perhaps Clive had other special talents. If he did, I had a feeling none of them were ones I would appreciate. "Lady Nestra, she likes a project. Likes to take on things no one else will touch, shine them up, turn them into something special. This place here, tweren't nothing but a field of rubble afore she came along. My lady, she designed everything you see here, spared no expense."

"Impressive. You came with her to Renga?" I asked as we mounted the steps to the palatial home.

"Naw. I was working one of the mens' clubs downtown, got caught stealing from the till, I'm not ashamed to tell it now. Our lady, she found me on the corner, beaten to half my life. Took me in on the spot."

"Did she?" I mused, surprised. I'd heard a lot of things over the years about Nestra Laroche, but her having a heart of gold hadn't been one of them. Saving a man, though, that was a good way to secure loyalty.

"Aye, she did," he leaned in, whispered conspiratorially. "See, she'd been visiting the club that day angling for an invitation. But they wouldn't let her in. It's men only, see. Made our Lady mighty mad, that did."

"I bet it did. So she saved you, then?"

"Aye. She believes in what's called equal opportunity. Promised me all the food and comfort I could want if I told her everything I knew about the club. Together, we'd have our revenge on the men as tossed us out, she said. And I dare say we have, now as she's in charge."

"What a grand story," I said, watching him pull a bell by the door. It wasn't lost on me that he didn't just walk in. For all his talk about her fine treatment, he was still not one of the household.

The home made use of the same dark marble as the fountains for its accents, twisting columns set against rough bricks of brilliant white. The door was made of wide wooden planks darkly burnished to match the columns on either side. Considering the lengths Lady Laroche had gone to securing the property, I was a bit surprised to find such a weak entrance, but then I tasted it. The briefest hint of magic leaving a metallic tang in my mouth as my auric field brushed up against its field. Someone had lain a decent protective shield on the door. Impervious to fire. Shock-repelling. And...glamour weakening? I was glad I hadn't needed to use any sort of magical masking on myself, that I'd insisted on a legitimate postmark, rather than conjuring an illusion. Nestra Laroche was canny.

The door opened revealing a rather rotund man wearing, of all things, a monocle. He used said eyepiece to scrutinize me.

"Yes?" he demanded in a bored way.

"Package for Lady Laroche," Clive answered importantly.

"Special Courier," I said, holding up my arm for inspection.

"I can take it," Old Squinty said.

"No, sorry. Ms. Laroche has to sign for it in person."

"Yeah," sneered Clive. "Otherwise don't you think Sandy or I would have brought it up ourselves?"

"Fine," huffed Squinty, ignoring Clive's jab. "I will take it from here. You may return to duty. Run along." He waved off my escort with a little wave of his hand. I almost felt bad for Clive as he scurried away. Almost.

CHAPTER 10

breath of fire! grasped by a queen
words hazy, melt like anger

"This way," the man droned, clearly too bored for life.

He ushered me into the mansion and set off at a decidedly slow pace. Good thing, too, since I could barely remember to walk as my brain melted under the onslaught of color. Everywhere you looked, art pieces threatened to outdo one another. Riotous mosaics littered the walls, abstract sculptures stood in rows, and between them, vines ran like feathery boas. The floors themselves were difficult to process, each octagonal tile a different texture, different color, different pattern.

"Is the whole house like this?" I wondered out loud.

"I beg your pardon?" Squinty asked, but I didn't bother answering. I sensed his question had been more out shock that I dared speak to him than any desire to actually interact. Besides, as we passed room after room off the great hall, I could see for myself that the carnival atmosphere never abated.

We stopped outside a wide set of doors. Squinty rapped twice and we waited. Just when I would have been tempted to knock again, a throaty voice called us in.

Squinty quietly pushed open one door, straightened his monocle and announced me. "Your package has arrived, Lady Nestra."

"Wonderful, wonderful." A tall, gorgeous woman walked towards us. I could only watch in wonder. The room was different from the rest I'd seen. Still colorful, but simpler. More sensual. This was a room made for pleasures, for relaxing, reclining and whatever else your mind could think of. Sheer scarves in every color of the rainbow hung from the impossible tall ceilings to billow gently in the wind like willows. Pillowed settees adorned the floor to create haphazard seating areas while the walls of the room were covered in row upon row of books. Above, the ceiling had been painted a bright turquoise blue dotted with white clouds. Nestra Laroche, gowned entirely in black with kohl-rimmed eyes and hip-length hair to match, wove her way towards us like a jungle cat. "Oxby, leave us," she ordered, a hungry look in her eye.

Did she think I was the package?

I started to protest, but Oxby had already shut the door behind me. When I turned back, I came face to face with Lady Laroche. Up close, she was older than I'd first thought. More worn. Frown lines marred her forehead and mouth: I could see that this was a woman who pouted when things did not go her way.

"Special Delivery for Nestra Laroche," I said, determined to stick to my script. Still, even as I dug the delivery out of my pack, I couldn't help staring around me, at the scarves, at the sky, at everything. She saw my gaze and smiled.

"I couldn't help bringing a bit of home with me," she said, pointing up at the ceiling. "As beautiful as your skies are, I miss my rainbows."

"Rainbows?" I asked. I could count the times I'd seen them on one hand. They were a rare event under a sky where light came from every angle, despite our frequent rains. Their beauty had always fascinated me. I kept prisms in my own windows to create tiny spectrums of light that would dance throughout the apartment.

"Yes." Nestra rubbed her hand together, reached for the package in my hands eagerly as she changed subjects. "This is for me?"

"Oh, yes. But you need to sign for it. Here." I thrust my pad towards her and the pout I'd suspected emerged.

Quickly, she scrawled her name across the three lines and passed the pad back to me. Before I could blink, she'd ripped the tube out of my hands, barely sparing the outside a glance before she was tearing into it.

"You should join me, you should... Ah!" Her hand had clasped around mine, and she half collapsed onto the nearest settee, pulling me down with her. Before I could argue, the words dried up in my throat. A crimson mist had begun to seep from the cylinder, hanging weightlessly like a mid-level gas. Blood red, vibrant and slightly sacrificial looking. "Here it comes. The stuff of dreams. The stuff of life. Better than sex," she muttered. She leaned forward, sniffing the air like the mist was the most fragrant flower and closed her eyes, smiling. She breathed in, and the mist climbed the air towards her, disappearing into her nostrils. The mist began to disperse and she started breathing more deeply, holding the tube up to face and burying her head in it, sucking the air out of it so that it caved in around her cheeks. When she emerged she was laughing, a deep throaty sound, like a lounge singer on a bender.

"Sorry, I didn't leave you any, dear." She stroked my cheek with ice-cold fingers and looked into my eyes. Shocked, I drew back. Her dark eyes had gone red, scarlet as the mist. Her hand fell to the cushion beside her and she sank down, her eyelids drooping. "And I'm afraid I'm going to have to leave you now, too."

"What was that?" I whispered. "Should I get you someone? Oxby, maybe? Your hands, they're so-"

"I'm fine, dear," she chuckled. "Can't you hear the music? Look, the rain has stopped! We're sure to have some rainbows now, don't you think, Eva? Such a marvelous party. Shall we dance? Come, let's." Her lashes fluttered, and then her face went slack. Eyes still open, still eerily lit from within like the devil's own nightlight, but no pupil response. She wasn't dead though, far from it. Her pulse was steady, strong. My best guess? She was in a trance.

Was this the feed? No wonder the police couldn't find any traces of the drug, I thought as I snatched up the letter and examined the emptiness within – this was a spell. Pearce was right. Magic was involved.

And now, so was I. Dammit. I was going to have to call in the Enso.

I stuffed the empty tube back into my pack. Hopefully, Nestra would assume that Oxby or one of her other minions had thrown it out. Pearce hadn't been able to find any clues on other letters but maybe the Circle could. They had deconstructionists who lived for this sort of thing, witches who excelled at magical forensics. I detected nothing amiss with the cylinder, but then, I wasn't part of the Enso. Magic wasn't my life. It was a simple extension of my natural abilities, like walking, talking, breathing.

Gently probing Nestra with my own magic, I sensed that while her body was here her mind was far, far away. Like, in another time. If I had to guess, the spell had taken her deep into her own memory banks. I took one last sweep of her vitals, deemed her healthy enough and started to rise. Remembering the health training I'd had years ago in school, I knelt at her side one last time and turned her on her side, propping her there with some pillows.

There. I had no idea how long the effects of the feed would last, but at least she wouldn't choke on her own vomit. Satisfied, I stood and left Nestra Laroche to her rainbows.

CHAPTER 11

poor loving soil
flowers bloom in dark places
wet with happy tears

My last drop off in Chalinex City wasn't far from the precinct. I came back through the middle-class suburbs, heading south this time rather than back west. I would have thought that coming back into the grime of the city from the 'burbs would have been unpleasant, but after seeing Nestra Laroche's home I felt dirty in a way I couldn't shake. At least here in the city the corruption was clearly visible. The Suburbs were clean and beautiful but their money was dirty in every sense of the word. Even their location spoke of entitlement: storms on this part of Renga almost always flowed in from the Northeast, which meant that the rich neighborhoods got watered and washed first, the clouds picking up dust and pollutants as they traveled, only to redeposit them on the rest of the city as they went. I was thankful Puraimura was northwest of Chalinex – a few degrees south and we all would have been bathing in their soot.

As I started to find myself in grittier neighborhoods, I felt compassion rather than disgust. The neighborhood I found myself in was the worst I'd seen yet. Sprawling tenements thirty stories tall, ecosystems of filth and decay, windows broken and cracked on almost every floor. Balconies designed for leisure now being used as drying racks for hand-washed clothing – items that had been laundered so often they had become devoid of color, dingy and ragged.

No wonder the inhabitants of Chalinex resented my people. At least we had the means to lift ourselves out of true hardship. What brought a person to live a place like this? Had they hoped to strike out on their own, build a homestead, only to get caught up in the rat race of city life? I may have had humble origins, but I saw now that I'd been blessed. I would never take my lifestyle in Puraimura for granted again. I'd known Chalinex had problems, but I'd never seen this part of the city, never realized. Truth was, most people here probably couldn't afford to send anything special courier. I imagined they didn't receive much, either.

As I traveled the streets, I was surprised to see more than a few kems – not just kets, like in Prime, but other hybrids. They looked comfortable here, if poor. No one stared at them, no one seemed to give them any trouble. I stooped to give one homeless ket some yendar, being careful not wake the child sleeping against his shoulder. Like Jonah, she had regular ears, though I could feel her magic. Would her eyes betray her when they opened, or were they also human enough to pass?

"Thank you," the man mouthed. I wanted to ask him why he lived like this, why he hadn't reached out the

Enso for help, but knew I had no right. It was not my place to ask, only to give. Still, I couldn't help wondering if the Enso knew magicals were suffering on the streets of Chalinex. Didn't we look after our own?

Troubled, I rose and walked on. Feeling hot with a swell of irritation, I pulled my hood down. I earned some whistles and purrs as I went, but no harassment. Here, at least, a girl could be herself. Squalor was an egalitarian mistress.

There were shops, but many of them were shuttered; the rest, half-empty. Corner markets with huge produce bins hosting bruised, sad looking fruits. Butchers with cases of sausages and offal, not a prime cut to be seen anywhere.

I didn't see a single pharmacy or medical clinic. Not one.

How did these people live? What magic had stolen their will? Here and there I spotted rebellious graffiti, but not as often as a place like this deserved. Everyone should have been rebelling, demanding better. We had an entire planet filled with quality arable land and all the great weather and cosmic radiation needed to grow abundant crops. There was no reason to live in squalor when the government would happily grant homestead rights to anyone ready to stake a claim. In Prime City, we had plenty of community action programs. These people, we would have found places for them, jobs, life with meaning.

Why stay here?

I just didn't get it.

I wasn't an organizer, though. Large groups of people? Not my scene. Still, I knew I'd be mentioning what I'd seen when I got around to visiting the Enso. The way things were going, it'd have to be soon, too.

A lot of the street signs were missing or spray-painted over, so it took me a while to find the building I was looking for. When I finally did, I cringed. This place was as far as you could get from Laroche's moat-encircled castle. Hell, it was the worst place I'd seen in Chalinex. And I was going inside. Had to, carrier's creed and all that, though a fiery star might have been more hospitable. I picked my way around several teenagers passed out on the steps and ventured inside. There was no security to stop me – the call box had been ripped off the wall and the glass doors were missing a key ingredient: glass. The mailboxes, amazingly enough, were intact. I guess in a place like this no one expected anyone to receive anything worth stealing. And here I was, carrying something, I didn't know what, valuable enough to require special delivery. Great.

I kept my hood down, all the better to hear and see. After pressing the elevator button several times, I sighed. Another broken thing. Of course.

At the end of the hall, a wide fire door was propped open, no doubt violating all sorts of safety codes. Shaking my head, I stalked towards the stairwell. It was dark inside and almost instantly my nose was assaulted with an unholy mixture of bodily fluids and stale smoke. My eyes teared from the fumes, but at least I could see well enough to avoid stepping in anything too disgusting. Believe me, being a ket has its perks.

I started counting off levels as I ascended, climbing towards my quarry on the eighth floor. One. Two. Three. I was just leaving the fourth floor when I heard a dull thud above me, followed by muffled voices and laughter. Senses tingling, I went on full alert.

"Come on, Rae, get up, you dog!" "Are you just going to lay there and take it like some bitch?"

More laughter, more thuds. And moaning, followed by a low keening.

"Aw, look, the dog's pissed itself!" a girl laughed. "Here's what happens as when a mutt tries to blend in with its betters." I heard a sizzling sound, like water being tossed on a campfire, and knew whatever was happening had just gotten worse.

Silently, I dashed up the stairs, taking three at a time. Long legs and feline reflexes made it easy. But they didn't prepare me for what I was about to see.

Three boys and a girl circled another teen who lay in a puddle of fluid on the floor. Piss, the girl had gotten that right. Two of the boys had their feet on the one I assumed was Rae – one with his boot on the side of Rae's head, the other with Rae's wrist under his heel. Everyone's attention was on Rae, and for a brief moment, we stared into each other's eyes. Then, the girl held a cigar to the back of Rae's pinned hand and his skin sizzled and steamed once more.

My fists clenched in fury. This wasn't my fight, I didn't know Rae from Sunday, but I'd be damned if I was going to let this continue. I summoned the powers of air and water, drew the moisture on the floor up into a swirl of punishment, drenching each of the bullies in their victim's own urine. The girl shrieked, dropped her cigar, rounding on me in fury.

"Get her!" she cried, and the other boys leaped towards me ready to fight. As if they could take down someone like me. I laughed and drew up all the piles on trash and filth I had passed below and sent it flying in their faces. Pa had always taught me not to rely on magic alone, so I didn't.

I aimed a fist into the first one's solar plexus, then took him out with an uppercut to the jaw. I barely missed an oafish jab from the second – clumsy, but it would have done some damage if it had touched me, considering the difference in our sizes. Not taking any chances, I went straight for his groin, sent him crying to the floor. The third was smarter than the others, maybe, and took a couple of steps back as I advanced. Furious, the girl pushed him towards me.

"What are you afraid of? She's just a girl. A kem, like him," she sneered.

His eyes darted between his friends and me, and then he shook his head. "Screw this, man. I'm out of here." He ran back onto the fourth floor and I heard a door slam in the distance.

"Coward." She spat on the floor, just missing Rae's face.

"Bully," I said quietly. "I think you'd better apologize."

She laughed, an oddly duck-like sound. I raised an eyebrow and she stared me down. Someone really needed to bring this princess down a notch. Smiling, I shrugged. "Okay. You win."

Triumph began to spread over her face,

"Rae? You should probably move." I gave him a small nudge of power towards the wall, and understanding lit his eyes. Quickly, he scrambled back, just in time to miss the flood of filth I'd summoned from above. Like a wave, garbage and waste crashed into her, knocking her to the ground.

She was still screaming when the guy I'd kicked in the nuts stood and dragged her from the landing. The first guy remained unconscious, but a quick scan of his vitals assured me he'd be okay.

I went over to help Rae stand. His vitals were good, but there were broken bones and burns. And my healing powers, well, they only really worked with Jonah. Purring could speed up any humanoid's cellular healing, but it wasn't an instant kind of thing. Poor Rae would have to heal on his own time.

He stared at me, eyes wide. Then, he looked down, embarrassed, only to find his pants unnaturally dry.

"You- How-"

"Magic," I winked. "You don't have any?"

I examined the peaked ears on his head. Similar to mine, but he smelled different. And his nose was wider, darker, flatter than the rest of his ebony skin.

"Wolven," he said, explaining. "Not ket."

"Ah," I said. "That explains some things. But those kids, they meant business. Especially that girl, she's nasty."

"Shari? She's not always like that. We used to be friends. I thought, maybe, well, we haven't talked in a while and I thought..." He trailed off. "I stopped by to say hi and she was hanging out with those guys. They started making fun of me. And her. That's when she got mad. I don't think she meant for things to get so out of hand."

He was shaking, going into shock, I realized. And dreaming, too, if he thought that girl was anything other than a banshee.

"Look, Rae, I'm going to give you some advice. Steer clear of that girl. You could have died today. You don't know what might have happened next if I hadn't come along. Do you live here?"

He shook his head and I exhaled, relieved. "Thank Buddha for small favors. Get home. Stay away from Shari and her goons. And please, sign up for some self-defense lessons. This city's a shithole. My advice? Finish school and get yourself over to Puraimura as soon as you can. We can always use some good runners at the PGPS."

"Really?" His eyes went wide. "You think they'd take someone like me?"

"Sure, why not? They hired me, didn't they? Just ask for Nikta Kozan when you come. And if you need help, here in Chalinex, go find my brother Jonah at Precinct 8. He's a good guy."

"A cop?" he asked with distrust.

"I know, I know. Cops," I rolled my eyes. "But he's good, I promise. Now get home, before I have to knock some sense into you, too." I grinned and the ghost of a smile passed his lips. Quickly he bowed in thanks.

"I will. Thank you, Ms. Kozan. I won't forget you!" He said quickly and fled down the stairs. Laughing, I leaned over the railing, watching him run. It was a good thing I'd cleaned the stairs already or else he could have slipped. Still, I yelled after him.

"See that you don't! And watch your step!"

I watched until he was all the way down and then resumed my climb. The stairwell still reeked, with stains and crumbs every few feet, but at least the most obvious offenses were gone. I hoped Shari and her friends' had plenty of hot water in their apartments. Or not.

I found my recipients behind door 8-JJ, The Gunjabmis, an elderly couple and several young children. As I pulled my pad out for the man to sign, he yelled over his shoulder, calling for his wife. "Omma! Henry has sent another letter!"

"Your son?" I asked as he scribbled his name, Pablo Gunjabmi. I couldn't help but be curious about the parcel.

"Our grandson," Omma said, teary as her husband pried opened the oversized cylinder and clutched a handful of ceecees to his chest. "Our daughter, his mother, died four years ago."

"Cash?" I asked, surprised. "He sent hard currency? Why not just wire you the money?"

"The exchanges are corrupt, they take everything in fees, or claim less was sent than it was. Henry left two years ago, as soon as he was old enough to make a living. It took some time, but now he sends us money as often as he is able. For his brothers and sisters, you understand."

And I did. Heart swelling, I reached into my own pocket, pulled out the tip Lief had given me at Otto's, pressed it into her hands.

"I can't-" She tried to push it back.

"Please, take it. Someone gave me a tip," I said, laughing and maybe also crying, just a little. "I'm not supposed to accept tips. Please. Take it. It must be hard enough, in a place like this..."

"It is," she said sadly, but then she brightened. "But Henry is saving. In another year, he says he will be able to send for us, so we can all live together. He's on a ship now, but he sent us the most beautiful brochure of Perseus, you know, the island planet? Says he's put some money down there for a houseboat. Soon, it will be his. Ours. Theirs," she said meaningfully, looking at the children now huddled around the dining table where Pablo was already putting the money to good use for a mathematics lesson.

"Good. A life at sea with your family sounds like a dream come true. Do me a favor, keep them away from that girl on 4, Shari? I caught her and some thugs beating up a kid in the stairwell."

"I know her," Omma sniffed. "Nasty girl, always was. Tried to get her hooks into our Henry, but he wasn't interested. Don't worry, we don't let them out of our sight. And, I know it looks bad, now, but the neighborhood wasn't always like this. Time was, we were a real community. And we still look out for our own."

"Good, I'm glad to hear it." On impulse, I hugged her. "Ohalo, Omma. It was a pleasure meeting you."

"Ohalo, miss-"

"Kozan, Nikta Kozan."

"Nikta, lovely name for a lovely girl. Well. You'd best be off, then. Maybe we'll see you again soon." Hope and gratitude rang clear in her voice.

"Soon, yes. I hope so. Ohalo."

"Ohalo." She closed the door, and I turned, heading back into the stairwell. This time, the stench didn't bother me so much.

CHAPTER 12

answers cut like black diamonds
skittering across the floor

It was nearing the end of most people's workday when I got back to the police station. This time, when the big guy manning the front desk saw me he straightened and glared at me like I'd killed his best friend. And maybe I had. Indirectly, of course, but still.

I cleared my throat and approached, refusing to flinch under his gaze. "Detective Pearce? He's expecting me."

He made a face like he was chewing on something bitter but nodded. He picked up the phone and announced my presence. He pointed to some grimy seats by the wall and narrowed his eyes at me. "Take a seat, and keep your hands where I can see 'em."

I made some jazz hands and leaned defiantly against the wall by the entrance to the inner sanctum of the station. No way was I going to let this guy push me around. And those seats? Yeah, my coat didn't need to be subjected to that.

After winning a prolonged staring contest with the desk sergeant (didn't he know a cat always wins?) I barely had time to gloat before Pearce came striding in.

"Nikta," he said, all business. "Come with me."

He turned his back on me and I had no choice but to follow. "Nice to see you, too," I grumbled.

If he heard me, he didn't show it. He brought me into a conference area, a little brighter and more softly appointed than the interrogation room. Wooden tables and chairs; large windows overlooking the busy street outside.

"Have a seat," he said, gesturing at the round table. "Kozan!" he called, sticking his head out the door and beckoning before joining me at the table.

Hiding my surprise, I pulled a pencil and notebook from my pack. After my delivery to Nestra, I had started taking notes, writing down my impressions of what was going on. If I was going to visit the Enso later, I wanted to make sure I had all my facts straight. I couldn't leave anything out.

Besides, I hadn't been lying to Pearce the last time I'd been here. Writing poetry really was a nervous habit of mine, something I did whenever I was idle. I'd write on napkins at restaurants, carve words into sticks in the wild, put a pen to any paper nearby. The lines often flowed from me with barely any concentration, mindless as breathing. Other times, I could spend hours stringing haikus together to form a renga, long-form poetry dating back thousands of years. In Ancient Japan on Earth, poets would gather together for days of drinking and poetic styling, each one taking turn to add another haiku to the string of verses, always alternating three-line haiku with two-line verse. Some rengas had reached upwards of 10,000 verses. Mine were simpler: less focused on the seasons, since there were none in my world; more beloved of the daily life, the mundane, my present moment.

As we waited for my brother, I wrote one lone word at the top of a fresh page. I wrote in it kanji, the hieroglyphic form of Japanerican writing, reasoning that if Pearce was still learning hiragana he would know few if any kanji.

I stared at the word. *Answers.*

Would I get any here? I hazarded a look at Detective Pearce and didn't like what I saw there. Jaw clenched. Fingers drumming on the table. The man was on edge and I couldn't blame him. In one day, I'd been insulted, attacked, verbally abused. Someone had tried to blow Lyric Pearce up, and he couldn't just leave the city the way I soon would. This was his home, his work. His domain. That last part had never been in question. If he had to ride the city hard into to submission, he would, I was sure. I just hoped he wouldn't drag down the rest of us along the way.

My brother rushed in looking worried. I smiled at him, trying to put him at ease. Pearce brought the attention back to him with a brusque demand. "Well, Ms. Kozan? How did it go? I hope you did not run into any trouble."

"Not with Nestra, no. She was pretty friendly, actually. Invited me to join her," I answered, hastening to add, "which I didn't, of course!" when my brother looked at me horrified. "She signed for the package then ripped into it like she was starving and it held a twelve-course buffet inside. Before I could stop her, a red mist came up out of the tube and she breathed it in. She told me it was 'the stuff of dreams', better than sex, and then she passed out, fell into some kind of trance." I paused, blushing as I remembered how she had clutched me, petted my cheek.

"That's it?" Lyric asked, disappointed.

"Well, no. Before she passed out she said some stuff about the sun coming out, the rain stopping. I got the idea that she reliving a party on her home planet. I checked out the inside but it was empty, no trace of anything, like you said."

"Do you have it? The cylinder?" Jonah asked eagerly.

"No, um, her servant came in and told me I had to leave. I didn't want to look suspicious so I left it there," I lied. They'd already told me they couldn't trace the magic. Maybe the Enso would succeed where Pearce and his people had failed. But if I handed the cylinder over now, The Circle would never get their chance. I just hoped Jonah would not see through my story. Luckily, he'd always been the one to tell tall tales, not me, and he trusted me at my word.

I looked at Pearce, saw him studying me and rushed to move the story along.

"I did get a chance to probe Nestra with a bit of my own magic before Oxby came. Wherever her mind was, it was far, far away. Deep in old memories."

"So you are saying that Lady Laroche, second daughter of Vice Consul Tindare of the Spartan Legions of Earth, Widow of Lord Aganon Laroche, is a drug addict? And she is not involved in this drug ring?" He sounded like he didn't believe me.

"As far as I could tell. If she was involved in the ring, I assume she wouldn't have been jonesing as hard as she was when I got there. Any normal person would have waited for me to leave, right? At least now you have an idea of what you're dealing with. Though I really think you should get in touch with The Enso and-"

"No!" Lyric cut in, surprising me. Even Jonah looked at his superior with a furrowed brow. "I told you before. We don't know if they're involved-"

This time, it was me cutting him off. "Save it," I interrupted him, not wanting to hear more about how he distrusted the very organization designed to foster trust between our two races. "Look, there isn't much else I can tell you. So if we're done here?"

I placed my palms on the table, ready to get up. Lyric nodded, getting up quickly. "Sure, your brother can see you out. But Nikta, don't leave town just yet. Stop in tomorrow before you go."

He turned and left without waiting for an answer. "Conceited jerk," I muttered to myself as I stuffed my notepad back in my bag, forgetting Jonah was right there until he snickered. I glared at him and he put his hands up in surrender.

"Hey, at least he's not making you stay in lockup," Jonah joked as he rose from the table.

"Thank Tara for small favors. Speaking of staying over, I was wondering-"

"Yeah, look, I would totally invite you over," Jonah said, stumbling over his words, "but I'm having some friends over and, well, you see, they don't know I'm..." He trailed off, gesturing at himself and then me.

"Right. Sure, no problem. I was just going to say I already had a place to stay," I covered smoothly. "I thought we could grab a drink somewhere, but if you're busy I totally get it. Maybe we can get some tea before I leave town. Or not. Whatever. We'll just play it by ear, okay?"

The relief on his face was so obvious it stung. My eyes watered a bit like someone had just thrown salt in them.

"Okay. Yeah, sure, that would be great. Where are you staying?" He asked as he put a hand on my back and guided me across the station.

"Oh, um, with Jericha, you remember her?"

"Sumisu?" He asked and I nodded. "Yeah, I remember her! I thought I saw her at the market on Finch street a few months ago, but figured I was imagining things. So she's here, huh? You guys keep in touch?"

"Yeah. We write each other all the time."

I didn't mean for it to come out like a judgment, but it did. Jericha wrote me almost every week. Jonah sent me empty cards on New Year's and Zyzygy, the semi-annual alignment of Renga with its three moons. Mama used to tell me that Zyzygy was such a great party, even Yuki managed to show up on time. The mid-sized white moon had an irregular orbit, erratically crossing our sky on a different path every few days. When it aligned with Hokku, Sakura and Renga, our magnetic fields shifted enough to trigger huge, drenching rains that would travel the entire planet. My ancestors had started a tradition of prayer and dancing in the rain to celebrate the green bounty that always followed.

Dancing led to sex, and sex led to babies, so Zyzygy had taken on some definite associations with fertility over the years, too, and a lot of babies could trace their conceptions to the three-day event.

"Work keeps me really busy," he started.

"I'm sure it does. Look, you don't have to explain. I didn't mean anything by it. You asked if we keep in touch, and we do. I'm looking forward to seeing if her place matches the image I've grown in my mind." Having seen most of the city today, I imagined it would not. But I kept my unfavorable opinion of Jonah's new home to myself. Still...

"Jonah, I was over on Zenta Road this afternoon and-"

"You went there? That place is really dangerous, Nikta! Mail gets delivered under escort there. Who the hell ordered a special delivery? Was it part of the drug ring, do you think?" he asked eagerly.

Smiling, I remembered the Gunjabmi family. "Definitely not. Just some grandparents, taking care of way too many kids. The eldest grandchild sends them back money and-"

"You were carrying hard currency?!" he exclaimed. I imagined his expression mirrored my own when I'd found out the same thing and chuckled.

"Yeah. Don't worry about it though. I'm fine, as you can see. But that wasn't the problem. That whole area, Jonah, it's a mess. I had to step in and save some kid from getting the stuffing knocked out of him in the hallway. And the building, I've never seen anything so dirty, so decrepit. It looks like it could fall down any minute, and their front doors are all busted in. Don't you guys have any presence in that neighborhood?"

Jonah shook his head, looking guilty. "No. It's not our precinct. There are two stations in the Mudlands but from what I hear most of the cops there are either on the take or too scared to do their jobs."

"Well, it sucks, Jonah, it really does. You know it's the only place I saw other kems walking around like they felt at ease? Tell me that's not the reason the city turns a blind eye there."

"No, of course not!" He had the decency to blush and look offended. "It's just the bad part of town. Every big city has one."

"Not Puraimura."

"Prime doesn't count," he said. "It's barely even a city."

"Only because all the immigrants can't stomach our kind. And people like you leave. We're getting smaller every day. And this city, this haven you call home now? It's a cesspool. At least have the decency to pretend you're trying to do something about it."

"I am, Nikta," he hissed, steering me away from the eyes of his fellow cops. "More than you, anyway. What do you do, that's better than me?"

"I deliver hope," I said. "But you seem to have forgotten what that means. Whatever. Have fun with your friends tonight. Although I think you should take a moment to consider what kind of friends they are if they would turn their back on you just because our people are different – differences that allowed us to make this world livable in the first place. Think about that – about where you come from. Think about what our parents would say."

Before he could stop me, I kissed him briefly on the cheek and fled from the station.

CHAPTER 13

laugh, hug, drink, eat, talk
sands of time cannot erode
the truest friendships

I walked aimlessly, my hurt and fury distracting me as I went until finally I realized I had no idea where I was or how to get to Jericha's flat. I stopped at a noodle shop, ordered some takeout so I wouldn't show up empty-handed and got directions to her place. Jonah probably had seen Jericha at the market – according to the map the waitress had drawn for me, her place was just around the corner from the north end of the plaza. At least it wasn't near the tenements. I had a feeling that as bad as it had been during the day, it would be even worse when people got off work and streamed towards taverns.

I assumed Jericha would be home. According to her letters, she only went out dancing or drinking on the weekend, a two-day event that came around only twice a month on Renga. Not that she wanted to live so austerely – she just couldn't afford anything more than that. Since we were already more than halfway through the month, I knew she'd probably be resting at home, listening to stories on the airwaves or maybe penning me another letter. I thought about calling her to warn her of my arrival. It would be the polite thing to do, but I couldn't resist surprising her. I hadn't seen her in far too long.

The front door of her building was locked, but when I flashed my PGPS bangle at a woman coming out she smiled and held the door open for me. See? Being in the PGPS was better than being a rock star: you got all the perks without the pain of fame. I rode a working elevator up to the fourth floor and stepped out. Unlike what I'd seen in the Mudlands, the halls here were clean and well lit. Nothing fancy, but still, the differences were stark. I counted three doors in the hall, each marked with their own letter. I would have known Jericha's flat even without the large C emblazoned in yellow paint upon the wood. The entrance had been trimmed in brilliant fabric flowers of purple and gold, hand painted and strung to resemble a qualitchka vine. The sole source of one of the galaxy's most expensive perfumes, prized for both its complexity and rarity. The vine took sixty years to reach maturity and then would bloom only once. The seeds had a short window of viability during which they had to be tended diligently in just the right conditions, while the mother vine swiftly withered away. The dried stalks and leaves were often used in teas believed to hold curative properties, but the flowers were almost always sold to one of two perfumeries, each ruthlessly dedicated to their olfactory pursuits. The roots, I'd heard, had long been rumored to induce hallucinations when prepared the right way, but that knowledge had been lost so long ago that most believed it to be pure superstition.

Jericha's grandmother had often told us legends of the vine from her home planet, seated under a trellis of her own heirloom plant: a dowry gift. She'd enchanted us with folk tales about the tiny tribes of fae-like beings it was believed to house inside its thick grey bark. We'd watched the carefully nursed plant bloom one fragrant night when we were ten, clapping as it released puffs of iridescent pollen, but the truest magic I'd experienced was the sheer headiness of its fragrance. Jericha and I each had our own adolescent vines now to care for from the seeds of that plant, and I hoped I would live to see them bloom someday. After the week I'd been having, I had to admit it was starting to look questionable.

Which made me look forward to seeing my friend that much more. I strode forward, rapping loudly on the door.

The door swung open and a pretty girl opened the door. I knew Jericha had two flatmates and recognized this one immediately by her green-tipped ears and kind brown eyes.

"Lindsey? Hi, I'm a friend of Jericha's. Is she home?"

Before Lindsey had a chance to answer me, my friend's own tell-tale blonde head popped up over the couch behind her. "Is that Jesse?"

"No, it's-"

"Oh my gods, Nikta!" Lindsey yelled, scrambling off the sofa and barreling towards me.

"Surprise!" I grinned, opening my arms and staggering backward as she threw herself into them.

"-your friend," Lindsey finished, grinning. She eyed me over Jericha's shoulder. "And yes, Jericha is home, as you can see. Anyway, I was just headed out. Nice to meet you though, finally."

Lindsey shook my hand and eased out the door past us. Jericha locked the door after her and grabbed my hand, pulling me with her towards the sofa.

"I can't believe you're here, why didn't you tell me you were coming? Jesse's going to be here soon, you'll finally get to meet him. Have you eaten? I already had dinner, but there's plenty of stew left for you if you want some. I can't believe you're here! How long has it been, two years?" The questions tumbled out of her in a landslide, as she dragged me down beside me, grinning like an idiot. Not that I was judging, since I was beaming right back at her.

"Two years, three months, I think."

"Too long," she said, pursing her lips. "But you haven't answered any of my questions! Why are you here?"

"The home office was short on carriers, so I took on part of a friend's delivery sector. And no, I haven't eaten. Here, I brought noodles!" I handed her the package. "I've been out delivering packages all day in the city, figured I'd spend some time with my favorite ket before heading home."

Jericha hugged me impulsively. "Aw! Well, I'm glad you came, even if you didn't give me any warning." She hopped up. "Come on, let's get you fed." She looked at the bag in her hand and seemed to melt. "Yan's Noodle Shop? Maybe I'm still a little bit hungry after all."

The galley kitchen was too small and narrow for two people to fit comfortably, so I sat down at the dining table while she took out some bowls. "Just so you know, Yan's stuff is amazing but I also have bouillabaisse, just the way my ojisan used to make it."

Remembering the delicately herbed fish stew her grandfather had often made, it was my turn to melt. "Oh, your soup, please. I'll have the noodles in the morning."

"I thought you might say that." She grinned and spooned the stew into a large bowl, balanced a wide slice of artisanal bread along the edge and slid the meal towards me. I dug in, taking a moment to appreciate the flavors.

"This is amazing. Thank you, Jericha."

"Glad you like it," she smiled, sitting across from me and pulling her own bowl in front of her. For a few minutes, we didn't speak, just enjoyed our meals. Though it had been years, we settled into our friendship with ease. "Now tell me. How is everyone at home? And your brother – have you seen him? You should have brought him, I keep meaning to look him up but, well, you know how it is."

"Yeah, life gets in the way, I know. I did see him, I saw him at the precinct, but trust me, you're not missing anything. He's still angry about the Olympic scouts, can you believe it?"

"Well, he was our best swimmer," she said gamely. Jericha had always had a thing for my brother, but he'd had a rule about not dating my friends. I think he'd done it mostly so that I wouldn't date his friends, either, but I hadn't minded. Why would I want to date a jock when I'd had one dogging my steps since my very first breath?

I looked at her over my bowl of soup. "Seriously? He knew the rules as well as anyone."

"Yeah, well, rules were made to be broken, don't you think?" she said, edgy. She stood up, went to the kitchen and came back with a bottle of cold rice wine and two small cups. "It's not fair," she said, pouring us each a glass. "We're good enough to work for the Front, good enough to settle worlds for them, but we can't compete in something like the Olympics?"

"Whatever," I shrugged, clinking my glass against hers and savoring the sweet sake. "It's not like kems can't play on private leagues."

"Sure, soccer, spaceball, the Air Derby. But when it comes to a lot of things, we're still second citizens."

"Yea, I know what you mean. I had to deliver a package to the Mudlands today. It was awful."

Jericha gasped. "You went to the Mudlands? No one goes there." She grabbed my hand. "How did you make it out?"

"Make it out?" I laughed, refilling our tiny cups. "You make it sound like the seventh circle of hell." Jericha made a face and I sobered up. "Seriously, it wasn't *that* bad."

"I don't know," she said, knocking back her sake in one smooth motion. After, she shook her head so that her blonde hair fluffed out in all directions, easily hiding her tall ears. She'd always worn her hair long. With her ears on the smaller side, she could pass for a reg if she wanted to. I wondered how often she tried, then tried to ignore the idle thought. "You don't live here. You haven't heard the stories."

"Well, it wasn't pretty, I will grant you that. I ran into some nasty kids, had to teach them a lesson. But there are good people there, too. Really good people," I said, thinking of the Gunjabmis.

She shuddered. "I can't imagine having to live there. I'm so lucky I met Lindsey and Reno when I moved here. Otherwise, I never would have been able to afford a place like this. As it is, we barely make ends meet."

"Then why live here at all? You know the rents in Puraimura are reasonable. Why live somewhere that seems so hell-bent on making people struggle?"

"Wow, you really haven't seen the good side of Chalinex yet, have you?" she said, laughing good-naturedly.

"You mean where the rich people live? Yeah, I've been there." I sucked a noodle from my spoon and frowned, remembering how Nestra lived. Even her vast wealth couldn't hide her loneliness. "I don't know if I'd call it the good side, though."

"You went to the North Bank?" Jericha gaped at me and filled our glasses again. Though they were small, I knew I had better start to pace myself or before long I might be passed out on the floor.

"I had a delivery to make. I'm pretty sure I saw most of the city today. Jonah's precinct, the wealthy burbs, North Bank, Mudlands, here," I said, ticking the districts off as I went. "I didn't really love any of it. The noodles aren't bad, at least."

"How was it?" she asked, setting her bowl down and stretching out on the floor in front of me. She'd always been like that – needing to move and stretch all the time, randomly assuming different yoga poses whenever she had to stand in line. "The North Bank is supposed to have some serious swank. I keep meaning to take a walk over there, but I never seem to find the time. Plus, I've heard stories about people getting harassed by the cops if they don't look like they belong."

"They should be patrolling the Mudlands, fixing it up, not bothering people who want to sightsee. Jonah and I argued about that earlier, too." I sighed, staring into my empty bowl. Empty, in so many ways.

"You're right, I suppose. There is a lot of corruption here. But there's a lot of beauty, too. Really, I swear, there is. There are people here from all over the 'verse. And kems, Nikta, all kinds of kems. Not just kets like us."

"Yeah, but don't you get harassed a lot? The looks I got on the street today... One guy called me yokai."

"You can find jerks everywhere, even Puraimura. Besides, how else can people get used to us if we hide at home or in places like the Mudlands?" She sat up, raising her arm over her head and leaning to one side as she winked at me. "Consider me your friendly Prime Ambassador."

"Well, when you put it that way," I grinned. "I can't think of anyone better to represent our people in the big city. You feel safe here, though, right?"

"Safe enough. All the violent crimes happen in the Mudlands. Although I heard there was some kind of an explosion at one of the police stations today."

"That was at Jonah's precinct, I was there."

"No way!" she exclaimed. "And you're worried about me? Gods, is Jonah okay?"

"Yeah, we're fine. One guy died, though."

"Wow, that is so terrible." She shuddered. "I can't imagine working in a place like that. I am so happy I studied fashion. My boss can be a pain in the butt sometimes but the most dangerous thing there are my fabric scissors."

"They are really sharp," I agreed, remembering how her prized possession could slide through thick suede like butter.

"Yes, they are. I'm glad you weren't hurt. In the explosion, I mean. Did they catch the guy who did it?"

I shook my head. "No. Actually, they-"

Someone knocked on the door and Jericha hopped up, interrupting me. "Hold that thought. This should be Jesse. I can't wait for you guys to finally meet." She bounced over to the door and opened the three locks. Seeing the man on the other side, she squealed and threw her arms around him, locking him in a long kiss. Finally, she came up for air, pulling him inside and bolting the door again. For all her talk, I couldn't help thinking a truly safe neighborhood wouldn't require so many bolts.

"Nikta, this is Jesse Tagazzi. Jesse, this is Nikta Kozan, my very best friend from Prime."

"The carrier? Cool. Nice to meet you," he said, sinking down onto a nearby chair. "Way Jericha tells it, you've been all over." He eyed me, staring at my ears a little longer than I would normally consider polite. For a ket, staring at someone's ears was a bit like ogling one's chest -- not only was it a bit rude to stare, but they were a highly sensitive area for any ket. As I am sure he must have known from dating Jericha, even if he was a reg.

"Sure, I've seen my fair share of Renga. But this is the first time I've been in Chalinex since I was in school."

"No way, really? Why?" His tone implied he thought Chalinex was the only place worth living.

"Just never had the calling, I guess," I said, deciding to evade any discussion about the merits of the city.

"Nikta's a country girl, she likes camping, that sort of thing," Jericha explained as she handed Jesse a bowl of bouillabaisse.

"Camping? Like, in the woods?"

"Woods, wilds, whatever. I grew up hitting all the trails around Puraimura when I was a kid, I love being out there. But I love my apartment, too."

"Especially her garden. You should see all the things she has growing in there. I miss that about home."

"Having a garden?" Jesse asked.

"That, and just the fact that we had the space to have a one if we wanted. Everything is so cramped here. Sometimes I feel shut in, even if we do have these windows." She waved a hand at the glass behind her.

"No wonder." I wandered over to the windows. Jericha's qualitchka trailed up along one side of the glass bolstered by a trellis and I noticed it had lost some leaves. "You can barely see the sky. There are so many buildings. I mean, look at this," I said, lifting up a drooping tendril of the plant. "Even the qualitchka is ailing."

"What are you talking about?" Jesse said, a mouthful of soup hindering his words. "You can see the sky perfectly well, it's reflected a thousand times in all the windows and mirrored 'scrapers."

"Sure, if you like seeing your sky cut up and rearranged into a thousand little mosaics, yeah, you can see it. Me, I like to see the stars how they really are."

Jesse grunted, focusing on his soup rather than engage further. Probably, he thought I was some sort of country bumpkin. I didn't mind. I was happy with the way I lived my life.

But I wondered. Was Jericha happy with hers?

CHAPTER 14

*drunken living – dreamy death
circles round at morning light*

We'd just polished off another small bottle of artisanal rice wine, a milky, mellow treat, when Jericha's other roommate came home.

"Reno, my man, how's it hanging?" Jesse held out a palm and Reno slapped it, followed by a complex sequence of fist bumps and shakes. Sometimes, guys reminded me of peacocks.

"Better now," Reno said, grinning as he held up a small green cylinder.

Jesse sat forward, rubbing his hands together, and Jericha cleared her throat loudly.

"Hey, Reno, you haven't met my friend Nikta. Nikta, this is my roommate Reno."

"Nice to meet you," Reno said, giving me a genuine smile. "Jericha talks about you a lot."

"Thanks, same. Good news?" I asked, nodding at the mail tube.

"You could say that." He winked and Jericha frowned at him.

"I've told you how I feel about that shit, Reno. I don't want it in the apartment."

"Aw, come on, sweetheart," Jesse cajoled. "It's not a big deal. You're not exactly living dry yourself."

"Sake isn't the same at all, and you know it," she hissed, and I started to understand just what might be in the letter. "Besides, we have a guest."

Reno had the good grace to look repentant. "Sorry, Nikta, I only ordered enough for me and Jesse. Next time, though-"

"The feed? That's what you guys are talking about?" I interrupted him.

"Yeah, everybody's doing it. It's not a big deal," Reno echoed.

"Not a big deal?" Jericha huffed. "People are dying, you idiots."

"Not from the feed. There are no drug traces in any of those deaths."

"Oh, sure, please, tell me again how people stop eating on their own all the time. Idiots. That red mist is some evil crap and I won't have any part of it." She poured herself another shot of sake, downed it, and then slammed another. "Besides, you both have work in the morning."

"Sorry, Jer, but you don't own me." Reno shrugged and tossed the cylinder in the air several times, catching it deftly. "You gonna join me in some safe non-toxic fun or what?"

"You know it," Jesse said. Almost as an afterthought, he apologized to Jericha, rubbing his hand along her thigh. "Sorry, babe. But it's really not a big deal. If you'd just try it-"

"Shut up." She flung his hand aside and stomped into the kitchen.

He shrugged and patted the seat next to him. "Come on Reno, I've got me a mind to visit Hokku tonight, without the space lag."

Reno laughed. "Now that is some choice fun, right there. But I've been reading this space thriller, where the girls are out-of-this-world hot. That's where I'm headed. I haven't had a foursome in weeks."

I gagged. "Hello, female sitting right here."

"Oh sorry, I didn't know you were game." Reno waggled his eyebrows.

"Ugh, no. Trust me, I'm not." But Reno wasn't listening. He and Jesse were huddled over the tube, Reno's hands gingerly breaking the seal on one end. And then the red mist was wafting out in a thin stream. As it rose, it split into two crimson streams, as if it could sense both waiting users. And maybe it could. This was strange, dark magic and I had no idea who or what had wrought it. The boys breathed in deeply, the haze disappearing into their noses and mouths. For a moment, I saw a flash of red in Jesse's dark eyes. Reno's were closed in ecstasy, his lips upturned.

"Oh, yeah, baby, I'd love to come inside. Introduce me to your friends. Don't worry, there's enough of me to go around."

"Pig," Jericha muttered. She tilted her head. "Come on, let's hang out in my room. Maybe they'll die in their sleep."

I picked up our glasses, following my friend. She had a fresh bottle of Sake in hand, this one full-sized. I looked back over my shoulder. Both men did indeed appear to be sleeping, though I knew they were tranced out under the vision-induced haze of the Feed. "How long will they be like that?"

"Hours. Days. Depends how much they took. If Jesse misses another day of work this month he's going to be fired. He's already taken three sick days." She sat down on her futon, looking up at me with tears in her eyes. "You know what kills me? This is his dream job. He worked so hard to get where he is now. It's just a medical sales job, but he loves it, you know? He loves talking with new people, loves feeling like he's part of something important."

"He works in medical – doesn't he get how dangerous the Feed is?"

"That's the thing. Most people don't think it's the drug causing the deaths. Until it's proven, people are going to keep at it. Who cares if some users are losing the will to live? Talk on the streets is that's just the losers, people who were better off dead anyways." Jericha poured us each shots and handed me a glass, clinking hers against mine before making a macabre toast. "Here's hoping they're right."

She tossed her drink back and I sipped at my own. "I don't think they are. Right, you know. I was at Jonah's precinct today, remember? This thing with the Feed, it's got the cops spooked. Me, too, if I'm being honest."

"Yeah. But at least you're in Puraimura. I hear it hasn't really caught on there yet?"

"Not that I've heard about. Though, you know me, I'm on the road so much..."

"Right. Well, hopefully, the cops will figure it all out soon. I know they say it's not toxic, but it's not safe, I don't care what anyone says." She looked at the door, and I knew she was worrying about Jesse. I couldn't imagine how much it must hurt to know your boyfriend would rather trance out in a dreamworld than spend time with you.

"They're on it, trust me." I decided to change the subject, not wanting the conversation to turn back to what had happened at the precinct. Knowing Reno and Jesse were involved with the Feed, I couldn't risk anything about my undercover work getting back to the wrong people.

I asked Jericha how her parents were, which led to some good laughs about her younger siblings, terrors of the playground. We drank some more, laughed a lot, and eventually, fell asleep side-by-side as we had so many times in our childhood: watching the play of our magic shine above us on the ceiling in a kaleidoscopic display of fiery red sparks and cool green shimmers of air.

My last thought before I passed out beside Jericha was that I couldn't put it off any longer. I would have to visit the Enso in the morning.

CHAPTER 15

*gemini watchers
are more than they say – but look!
the fog is lifting*

Reno and Jesse were still passed out when Jericha and I left in the morning. We shared a quiet breakfast at a local diner, my treat, and then parted ways. She, dashing off to a costume fitting for one of the opera singers at the theatre where she worked; Me, paying a call to the Enso. Pretty much every city on Renga had a local chapter that reported back to the original governing council in Prime. I'd heard grumblings that the Enso here in Chalinex considered itself above the rest, not surprising since the younger city had long outstripped Prime in terms of population and development. Today, I would find out for myself.

As a natural-born magic user, I'd been raised knowing the protocol for a visit. The first step was getting in. One did not simply arrive on the doorstep of the Enso and knock on the door. Knocking was for regs, and regs had to request their visits by appointment and go through a background check before admittance. The Circle had been threatened enough times by regs to warrant the extra security. My mother believed the protocol garnered the Enso more respect, too – if it looked like an embassy, acted like an embassy, well then, it must be legit.

The protocol for someone like me was simpler – all I had to do was pass a test. This was one of those Magritte-type situations where a door was not a door. It was a warden, a sentry, a litmus-test for magic. Heavily shielded against mundane entry or attacks, it ticked and hummed like an angry nest of clockwork wasps, the slowly turning gears within watching, waiting. Any display of magic would do, it needn't be fancy. Still, it never hurt to impress the Enzo. I closed my eyes and cracked my neck a few times, considering. And then I smiled. I exhaled slowly, my breath frosting on the air before me, washing over the door with an arctic effect. The gears stopped turning, freezing in place for a one moment, two – and then the door heated up with a blinding glow, the gears began to turn, and the door walked itself off its hinges to reveal the inner sanctum of the Enso. I took a confident step inside, and the door scuttled to shut itself behind me, cloaking the hallway in relative darkness. I slipped off my boots as a small, spiderlike automaton climbed off a nearby table, snapping its two front legs together to create a brilliant orb hovering above it, and it began to move in a jerky fashion down the hallway.

The Enso may have been a high council, but it did not rely on servants to open and close doors – why bother, when you could spell machinery to do basic tasks? The enchanted automatons were basic compared to the AI up on Hokku and elsewhere, but on Renga they always felt cutting edge. I tried not to look amazed and focused on following protocol. I knew the drill. Follow the bot. Receive an audience.

The spider stopped before a set of gates, made a few more gestures and clicks with its legs and leaped back out of the way. The golden, geared entrance folded in on itself neatly, pressing against the walls on either side of the archway to create an intricate design, levers and gears now resembling a bronzed sculpture of flowers and vines.

I shut my mouth and walked under the bower as if I saw this sort of thing every day. Here, the room was bright with the light of the stars above. Three of the walls, as well as the dome above, were made entirely of glass. No seams. No metal. Another space built by magic. I knew the council designed their offices with intention. Each space was meant to impress and cow the regs, make them appreciate the favor our kind did for them by policing its own. What most did not realize was that the spaces were also designed to balance our magic, to allow us to harness the elements more easily. It was this sort of attention to detail that made the Enso a force to be reckoned with, its agents the most powerful mages on the planet. My people, though I had had little contact with the Circle in recent years.

"Nikta Kozan," two sweet voices said in chorus.

I looked up at the women sitting comfortably at a wide table.

"Cousins," I said, inclining my head to hide my surprise. Ava and Vivien were the twin daughters of my great-aunt, my mother's first cousins, and ten years my senior. As a young girl, I had often sat for them as a living doll, allowing them to tease and braid my hair, make up my eyes. They'd taught me everything I knew about fashion.

And I hadn't seen them since Jiji's funeral.

They'd left Puraimura while I was still in school, long before Jonah's Olympic debacle, immersing themselves deeply into the magical world with high ambitions. Apparently, whatever they had been doing had paid off. To see them here receiving visitors could only mean that they had reached a position of some power, though I'd received no word of it. Idly, I wondered if they now fought over power the way they used to over eyeliner.

I bowed deeper and followed the opening script every ket on Renga learned by heart at an early age: "By the breath of magic, girded by the elements, I come to the Enso seeking balance."

"Please, Nikta," Ava drawled, rising to stand. "There's no need for formality here. Come, give your old cousin a hug."

I grinned, looking to Vivien for confirmation, and rushed to Ava, allowing myself to be embraced. She smelled the same as she always had, of cool water and lavender. When I came up for air, Vivien was waiting for her own hug. Where Ava smelled of peace and reflection, Vivien smelled of woodsmoke and spices.

Stepping back, I saw that they each had fine metallic strands woven through their ice-white hair: gold for Vivien, silver for Ava. The whiteness of their hair had little to do with age – kets didn't go grey the way regs did. Ava and Vivien had been born pale like their father, with alabaster skin and hair that emphasized their huge, dark charcoal-hued eyes. Vivien, always the one with a flair for drama, had rimmed her eyes entirely in deep lapis kohl, making them look larger than life. Her hair, like mine, was short and spiked. Ava wore no makeup that I could detect, her hair shimmering in long sheets down to her waist.

"It's good to see you," Vivien said, squeezing my shoulders before she let me go, scanning my face as if it held some unknown answer. And it might have, for her. Viv and Ava had always excelled at telepathy and mind games. My mother had always said they must have practiced in the womb before they could talk, so skilled they were at communicating without speaking.

"But why are you here?" Ava asked, gesturing for me to take a seat. "Surely it wasn't to see us."

"No," Vivien agreed. "She didn't even know we would be here."

"Reading me already?" I teased, the barest warning in my voice. They may have been my cousins, my elders, and important at the Enso, but the only mage I'd tolerate in my brain was me.

"No cousin, there is no need." Vivien's laugh beach chimes in the breeze. "Your face said it all when you entered."

"Aye," Ava agreed. "You wouldn't make it three days as a diplomat with that face. You always did have the most expressive eyes."

"Is that so? Well then, it's a wonder I lasted through the day working undercover for Precinct 8."

Vivien let out a low whistle and leaned back in her chair. "Precinct 8? The same one that was blown up yesterday?"

"Hardly blown up, dear," Ava chided.

"Attacked, then." Vivien waved a hand dismissively. She looked at me, her eyes fathomless. "There was a bomb, was there not?"

"Yes. There was. One I delivered." At their sharply indrawn breaths, I held up a hand. "Not intentionally, of course. I was running someone else's route, delivering the letter to the lead detective, Lyric Pierce. I was talking with Jonah when the parcel exploded, killing the detective's assistant."

"Jonah was there?" Ava asked.

"He works there."

"Ah – yes, I'd forgotten. So strange to think of our Jonah working in law enforcement. I would have expected him to follow a trade that would take him to the shore, on the water. Anywhere but here." Ava shook her head, looking mystified. "You just never know where life will take you, do you?"

"No, we don't. But I want to know more about this work Nikta is doing. What happened after the bomb was detonated?" Viv demanded.

"They blamed me, of course. If Jonah hadn't been there, I'd probably still be trying to talk my way out of a cell. Luckily, he was. But Pearce didn't let me off easy. He enlisted me to work undercover for them on an active case."

"The same case that motivated someone to try and kill this detective?" Viv asked shrewdly and I nodded. "And you agreed to this? Without contacting us first?" Her voice rose, and I nodded again.

"Peace, Vivien," Ava said, placing a hand over her sister's own. "Nikta is here now. Tell us, cousin, why have you come?"

"Well, the bomb, it was magical, obviously. Nothing else would have ever slipped past our sniffers in Prime. Even this, it shouldn't have made it. But things have been tight lately, people calling out of work, or quitting altogether. It's the reason I'm here this week in the first place."

"Interesting. And convenient," Ava said slowly, exchanging a look with Vivien.

"Yes, I'm beginning to think so, too," I agreed. The man I'm filling in for, I think must have been involved somehow. Getting paid off to carry drugs for some dealers, or at least not to ask questions. His wife just had a baby, and I imagine he was happy to earn the extra money. But he's been putting off coming back to work."

"Mmm. I hear parenthood does tend to make one reevaluate one's life choices from a higher standard," Viv said drily.

"My thought exactly." Viv and I had always seen eye to eye, though I'd always admired Ava's inner calm. "So, Detective Pearce has been investigating some drug, the Feed. Have you heard of it?"

"Unfortunately," Ava said, making a face. "Dream magic at its worst. Regular users get so addicted, they don't want to come up for air. People have died, starved themselves to death chasing the trances."

"Right. Well, Pearce is pissed. The cops can't figure out what is killing these people, how the drug works."

"They don't know it's magic?" Vivien leaned forward, intense.

I shook my head. "They suspect. But the Feed leaves no trace, as you probably already know."

"We have our sources on the force," Ava confirmed. "But no one has confirmed anything for sure."

"Well, I've seen it. Twice in one day, in fact. Pearce had me deliver a letter they intercepted under the suspicion that was heading to someone in the ring. Pearce was only partly right though – the letter itself was the delivery system for the feed. I watched Nestra

Laroche open the tube and trance out right in front of me."

Ava gasped. "Lady Laroche?"

"Who would have guessed?" Vivien said sarcastically. She'd never like people who put on airs.

"Yeah. And then, when I was at my friend's flat last night, her roommate came back with a letter from his source. Same deal – open the tube, red mist comes out, you inhale it, and then you start trancing out." I reached into my pack, pulling out the two cylinders I'd collected, handing one to each of the sisters. "The effects are almost instantaneous. Hallucinations set in within seconds, from what I can tell, and within minutes the users are completely tranced out."

"By the Buddha. You've given us more to go on in five minutes than our sources at the police have delivered in months." Ava rolled the tube in her hands, examining it carefully.

Vivien sniffed hers, handed it to Ava for inspection. "As you said – no trace of any drug or magic is detectable. No return address, either. And no fingerprints, I assume?"

"None."

"What did your detective think of this information?" Vivien asked?

"He is worried. But he still did not think he needed the Enso's help. I disagreed. Which is why I'm here. He doesn't know I kept the letter, he thinks I left it with

Nestra. And after seeing Jericha's friends, how it's affecting them and everyone around them, I knew I had to come first thing. So, will you help me get an audience with the Circle?" I asked earnestly.

This time, both twins laughed and I couldn't help feeling a little put out.

"But my dear," Ava wheezed, trying to catch her breath. Viv was still laughing heartily, her head buried in her lap. "We are the Enso. We assist the Arch-mage himself, and are his seconds in command, taking over his rule when he is away, as he is today. There is no higher authority in all of Chalinex."

Shocked, I stared at them both. "You?" I pointed at Ava and then Vivien. Finally, I broke down laughing. "They're trusting you? Why, our mothers barely trusted you to babysit, and now you have the run of the magical world?"

"I know," Viv giggled, straightening and wiping tears from her eyes. "It's amazing, isn't it? Ava has grown up enough for the both of us, enough to impress the Arch-mage. He just barely tolerates me."

"That's not true and you know it," Ava said seriously. "He is terrified of you, that is all."

"As well he should be," Viv rejoined with a feral grin. She turned that grin on me and I understood how the Arch-mage must feel. "Now. Tell us everything again, from the beginning. And don't leave anything out."

CHAPTER 16

plans shift like tracks in the sand
obscuring all clarity

It took me the better part of twenty minutes to fill them in, despite the fact that they barely spoke more than ten sentences. Every once in a while Ava would flick her eyes at Viv, who would then pepper me with a brief question or request for clarification. It had been a long time since I'd seen my cousins, but I fell back into the rhythm comfortably. The mindspeak might have made some people uncomfortable, but I knew they didn't do it to hide mean words or talk behind my back. It was just the way they were. Ava and Viv went together like yin and yang – so different, and yet one. Viv had joked that the Arch-mage merely tolerated her, but the fact was that without her Ava would probably never have left home. She was too cautious, too rational. Viv was fire, passion. The only thing that ever held her back was Ava – probably the only reason Viv had survived her wild youth.

"And so," I sighed, wrapping up my tale, "I came here. The police have no idea what they are dealing with, and even if they did, they're ill-equipped to handle it.

Someone is using magic in a way they shouldn't, which means this is a matter for the Enso."

"You did the right thing," Ava said, leaning forward and placing a hand on my knee. "But then, you always have."

Vivien nodded in agreement. "You always were wise, even as a child."

"Now, I have just one more question for you," Ava said, looking at me carefully. "Did you come here to pass off the problem to the Circle, or are you willing to do some work for us, as you have for the police?"

I swallowed, suddenly nervous. "Honestly?"

"You can always tell us the truth, you know that," Viv said.

"Undercover work isn't really my thing. I like my life." I watched the twins faces, but they gave no sign of what they might be thinking. "I'm not sure I want to dig any deeper into what's going on. But I don't think I can walk away, either. Too many people are being hurt by this," I said, thinking of Jericha, of Duffy.

"We would never ask you to do anything we think is too dangerous," Ava reassured me.

I peered back at her, familiar with her way of choosing words. Her inclusion of "too" did not escape me. "But it will be dangerous?"

"It may be," she acknowledged.

"But you can handle yourself. We've always known that. Just look at what you did with those brats in the Mudlands," Viv said, grinning.

"Brats, Viv," I reminded her. "Not crime lords. Not drug dealers. Teens playing at being tough."

"Still." She shrugged. "What you did in there was nothing short of amazing. Truly gross, but impressive."

"Yeah," I laughed, remembering the way the way Shari had been drenched from head to toe with filth. "It was pretty gross."

"And impressive," Ava reiterated. "Too call up that level of power, across that distance and focus it with such precision? Not all mages could have done what you did. And even fewer would have had the presence of mind to use their surroundings as a weapon. You may not have the inclination to look for trouble, but you know what to do when it finds you. I have absolutely no doubt that you can handle anything that comes your way. I never have."

Her smile warmed me, reminding me of my mother's for a moment. Then, her face turned serious again.

"So you will help us?"

"What exactly do you want me to do?"

"The same thing you did for the police, really. Deliver a letter." As Ava spoke, Vivien rose and retrieved a dainty, grass green cylinder from a table in the corner of the room. Vivien leaned over my seat and handed it to me, giving me a quick peck on the cheek.

"It's not a bomb, I promise," she whispered in my ear before straightening.

"Really, Viv, must you be so dramatic?" Ava complained, but her eyes were twinkling.

I turned the tube over in my hands, weighing it. "So, what is it?" I could detect no hint of magic, but that didn't mean anything. The best mages could make their spells dormant, undetectable until activated.

"A tracking letter," Viv said, perching next to me.

"There's a man we've been watching, Axel Lyell. We know he is connected to the drug ring somehow, though we have been unable to determine whether he is simply running interference for them with the other syndicates or if he is an actual dealer. We have refrained from direct interaction because we don't wish to tip our hand," Ava explained. Viv snorted, and Ava rolled her eyes. "A tactic not everyone agrees with."

"I still say we bring him in and convince him to talk."

"Axel is not of the magical community, therefore he is not under our jurisdiction," Ava said impatiently, as if she had explained this more than once before.

"Someone is making this drug using magic. That puts it within our sphere," Viv argued.

"Perhaps. But the regs do not see it that way. There are rules to be followed, protocols to observe," Ava said.

"People are dying," Viv countered in a low voice. "Kets."

"Even so," Ava said heavily. She turned to me. "Do you see why we need your help? You are working with the police already. They will not work with us, but you can. Right now, both sides are stymied, clueless how to proceed, locked in by their own rules and regulations. But you. You are PGPS. You can go anywhere. Reach anyone."

I tilted my head, pursing my lips. I exhaled, wondering if I would regret my next words. Because in my heart, I knew I had already agreed. I knew I would help them.

"What happens to him if I give him the letter?"

"Not enough," Viv grumbled.

Ava ignored her. "We'll be able to see and hear everything Axle does for twenty six hours. The magic in that letter will give Viv and me a one-way view into his mind."

"And what does it say? The letter?"

"Nothing, it's just an invitation to next month's gala." Ava winked.

"The Enso hosts galas?" I said, unimpressed.

"Once a year," Viv yawned. "We invite the city council, plus all the movers and shakers of Chalinex. It puts a shine to the act of civility between us and the regs."

"It needn't be an act, Vivien," Ava said quietly. "We are all just people, trying to live our lives."

"I know that. You know that. But them? I'm not always so sure." Viv said, looking disgruntled.

I couldn't help feeling they were both right.

"Okay, I'll do it," I huffed. "But I'm not saying this is going to become a regular thing. I'm not an undercover agent."

"Actually," the twins said, grinning at each other before turning to me. "You kind of are."

"Whatever," I said, rolling my eyes and stifling a smile. "Just draw me a map. I'm supposed to hit the road back to Prime today, and I still have to check in at the precinct and pick up outgoing mail before I leave."

"And come back here and give us a full report," reminded Ava.

"Yeah, right, that too," I said, my half-smile souring. At this rate, I would never get out of Chalinex City.

"Here, this where you need to go." Viv handed me directions written out in her distinctive scratch, the refined flairs and dips of Ava's calligraphy notably absent. "Just two lefts and a right. He's got a place on this side of the river, penthouse in a huge complex, you can't miss it."

"Okay." I stood, tucking the tiny invitation into my pack, tightening the soft leather straps before shouldering the bag. "Well, I guess I'll be seeing you in a little bit, then."

"Not without some love first, you!" Viv came round and hauled me into a deep hug.

"Take this, too, just in case," Ava said, placing both her hands on my shoulders as I turned to face her. A warm feeling filled me, igniting a tingling feeling along my skin. Just when I thought it was starting to feel uncomfortable, she released me. "Be safe, cousin."

"What was that?" I asked, feeling flushed.

"An auric boost. It should augment your powers nicely while making you slightly less impervious to physical harm. Think of it as a lucky shield."

"Neat, thanks." My tone was casual, but I knew what she'd just done was advanced magic. It was harder to mess with someone else's aura than you might have thought. Disturb an aura by agitating a person? Sure, that was easy. But to strengthen something that was normally fueled by that person's own connection to the planet's energy waves? That took a lot of power and no small amount of skill and focus. "Alright, well I guess I'll see you guys later."

Quickly, I kissed them both on the cheek and headed back out the way I'd come. Even though I knew I'd be back, it was hard to leave. I hadn't realized how much I'd missed them. Telling myself not to cry and tearing up a bit anyway, I looked over the instructions Viv had given me, turning left as I left the building. I walked for several blocks, took another left, then a quick right and continued on for some way until finally coming to Axel's building.

Viv was right. I couldn't have missed it. The building was an homage to modernity, covered with colorful pipes and external elevators. Everything shone with rainbow colors, the mirrored glass hiding the wealthy within. Because there was no question the people here had money. This may not have been one of the posh mansions across the river, but it was as close as you could get without actually being there. There were doormen at each entrance, as well as guards. Everyone going in and out was dressed impeccably. I received several sideways glances as I approached the door, but no one said anything outright.

No one, that is, until I opened my mouth to talk to the doorman.

"Service entrance is at the side," he said dismissively, flicking an invisible piece of lint from his coat and then staring pointedly at my dusty boots.

"Fascinating," I drawled, staring him down. Honestly, how boring and predictable could you be? "PGPS. I have a special delivery for a Mr. Axel Lyell."

I watched him come to attention as I dropped the name and flashed my calressium bangle.

"Certainly. My mistake. This way please."

He ushered me inside the building, escorting me past the guards and to the elevators personally. When the doors opened, a girl my age jumped to attention from where she'd been slumped against the wall.

"Zeddie, this young woman has a PGPS delivery for Mr. Lyell. See that she gets there straight away."

"Yes, sir." She bobbed her head up and down, becoming paler with each shake of her chin.

The doorman turned and left, and I entered the car. Zeddie eyed me, not with disgust but fascination.

"You really work with PGPS?" she whispered.

"I do."

"Zow. I wish I could do something exciting like that. See other places. Meet new people. Chalinex is so boring." She snapped the gum in her mouth.

"You should apply," I said, shrugging. "We always need more people."

"Even regs like me? I don't have any powers."

"Of course. The PGPS accepts all kinds. Apply – what's the worst that could happen?"

The doors opened and I stepped out.

"I could be stuck here forever," she whispered, and lift had gone and I was left standing alone in a long opulent hall of glass and golden carpet. There were only four doors along the hall, each flanked by two brass lanterns that shimmered dimly as if by firelight. Otherwise, the only light in the hall came from the stars outside, casting a warm glow over everything.

I took the Enso's letter from my pack, reading the apartment number again, and walked down the hall until I came to the fourth door. I had barely knocked when the door swung open. A young man looked at me through half-open, heavily lined eyes.

"You have something for Axel?" His voice was high, with a strange accent I couldn't place. An off-worlder, no doubt. The scorn in it for me was unmistakable, though whether it was because I was PGPS, a ket or a female, I couldn't tell.

"Yes," I said, showing him the letter.

"You can give it to me," he demanded, reaching for it.

"Sorry, no can do, I'll need Mr. Lyell to sign for this himself."

"Let her in, Rama."

"But Axel, you said-"

"I know what I said," Axel snapped, approaching Rama and cuffing him lightly on the back on the head. Rama winced and scurried from the hall as I stepped in.

"Please, you'll have to excuse my young lover. He's still in training." Axel's eyes roamed over my body as he hummed to himself. Instantly, I felt dirty but I fought the urge to shove the letter into his hands and back out of the house. I was PGPS, after all. I'd encountered worse.

"If you'll just sign here, I can give you-"

"No rush. Come with me, I have something I think you'll like." I blinked, astounded as he walked away. Was he going to offer me drugs? Try and woo me right now? But, I couldn't just leave the package. Perhaps he knew any real PGPS carrier would never do so, and this was simply a test. Sighing, knowing I had to see this through, I followed the jackal into his den.

The flat was pretty much exactly what I would have expected from a drug dealer. Dark fabrics. Black walls. Shining metal furniture. Not a piece of wood anywhere. I felt like I'd walked into an ancient vampire novella, and I didn't like it one bit.

He turned into his office, leading the way, and I followed. What I saw there made me gasp in surprise. This time, I did take a step back but quickly recovered. If he was trying to scare me, a ket, it had worked. The floor was carpeted with the hides of earthly felines. My ancestors, in a manner of speaking. Tigers. Lions, Cheetahs. Jaguars. None existed here on Renga, at least, not that I knew of, not unless some rich person had one as a pet.

"Beautiful, aren't they?" On the walls, paintings of big cats in the wild hung so lifelike it seemed they might jump right off the canvases. "I do so love felines. Of every kind." His voice dipped suggestively and I swallowed. Okay, well this was getting weird fast. He may not have wanted to skin me, but it was clear he wanted to add me to his collection. I scanned the area for magic, for something that might scream "I'm the source of the feed", but found nothing. I didn't feel a drop of magic in the vicinity. If Axel was selling the feed, he didn't seem to be making here.

"Ah," I stalled, now wondering if that the scorn I'd seen earlier on Rama's face had actually been jealousy. "That's great, I suppose you've come to the right planet then. You have great taste – in art, I mean. My husband would love these paintings," I said, dropping the none-too-subtle hint.

"Husband? I find it difficult to imagine what sort of man would allow his beloved to traipse around a place like Chalinex unescorted."

"Oh, um, Innis doesn't mind. We're both PGPS. Trained together. Anyhow, I have more deliveries to make, so if you don't mind signing..."

"Such a pity," Axel sighed, taking the letter from me and scrawling a large single "A" in my notebook.

"On the other hand," I said, deciding to fish for more information, "if you have an idea where a girl like me could score some of that new mind-candy, what's it called, the feed? I'd be ever so grateful. My husband's been begging me to bring some back to Prime, but I'm just so unfamiliar with this city..." I trailed off, trying to look doe-eyed and hoping he'd take the bait.

Axel's gaze went hard. Narrowing his eyes at me, he tapped the tube against one hand like he wished it were a larger baton, something that could do more damage.

"I think you'd better leave now."

"What? Did I say something wrong? I figured a rich guy like you...Innis told me everyone's doing it. Ouch!"

Axel's hand had clamped down on my shoulder and he was steering me roughly towards the door.

"I've a mind to report you to the PGPS," he snarled, shoving me outside into the hall.

"Oh please, sir, don't-" I cried, not really even needing to act anymore. If the PGPS thought I was doing drugs, I'd be out of a job. But it didn't matter. Axel had already slammed the door shut. For a moment, I wondered how I could have been so stupid. Then, I shook it off. I mean, I was working with Pearce and the Enzo. The PGPS would understand. They'd have to. Hopefully, he'd only been bluffing, anyway.

I rubbed my shoulder, grimacing as I made for the elevator. Was Lyell really just an innocent, run-of-the-mill sleaze? Or worse, had I had just burned the Enso's only lead?

CHAPTER 17

a leaf on the wind
buffeted between three fates
knows not where it goes

I was still shaking twenty minutes later as I collected mail from Chalinex's PGPS headquarters for hand-carrying back to Prime. I tried to focus, knowing it would be important for me to make friends here, now more than ever, but I had a hard time. More than one person noticed my unease, asked if everything was okay. Each time, I brushed them off with a reticent "family troubles," which seemed to appease everyone.

I wasn't lying. Jonah hated me, hated being ket. My cousins had drawn me deeper into their world of conspiracy, power, and politics. I'd started this trip wishing I was closer to my family and now I wondered if I'd been searching for comfort where it could never be found.

So, I kept the small talk to a minimum, barely processing the names of the people I met. It was rude, I knew, but I couldn't muster up a sense of calm or normalcy. My brain was on overload. I took the bundle of outgoing letters and small packages, noticing that the majority of them were ultimately heading off-world, with just a few things destined for Prime and other colonies on Renga. Officially, my work in Chalinex was done. My job now was to deliver the mail through the sorting facility in Prime, not make any personal deliveries myself.

Unofficially, however... I still had people to see and reports to give. Starting with Lyric Pearce.

When I arrived at the precinct, the skies were clear but the desk cop did a mean impression of an angry storm cloud as he glowered at me.

"You again. Didn't you do enough damage the last time you were here?"

The hair on the back of my neck rose and I resisted the urge to run a hand through my hair.

"That wasn't my fault," I said, shrugging. "Detective Pearce wanted to see me today."

"I'll bet he did. Way I see it, you're lucky you didn't spend the night in lockup. If it was me-"

"Well, then we're both lucky it wasn't you. Let Pearce know I'm here. I'll be over there." I gestured at some empty chairs far from the desk and stalked away.

We ignored each other for the next three minutes and twenty-eight seconds, the exact amount of time it took for Lyric Pearce to push open the door to the inner sanctum.

"Kozan, let's go." He held the door, his eyes an unreadable sea of green.

I eased past him, knowing if I'd had a tail it would have been twitching with agitation. Pearce didn't like me, I knew that well enough and it was okay. I didn't much like him, either. I wasn't sure he was trustworthy, cop or no cop. Jonah seemed to respect him, but these days that didn't mean much.

He ushered me into a private room, but at least this time it didn't appear to have been designed for interrogation or intimidation. If I'd had to guess, with its soft seating and coloring books in the corner, this was the room where loved ones were notified of progress on cases – a safer space where the worst and best of news could be broken.

I sat down in one of the cushy chairs at the table, a single piece of carved wood polished to a high shine and waited for the detective to take a seat. Instead, he walked to the large window and clasped his hands behind him as he stared up the sky.

Tic-toc, I thought.

"I did what you wanted," I said. "I delivered your letters and I reported back. Now, I'm here again. Why? You and I both know I haven't done anything wrong."

He cracked his neck, turned slowly. His gaze pierced me, and I stiffened, hoping he didn't know I had gone to the Enso against his wishes.

"You seem to be a good person. Your brother even says so, despite your obvious differences. That says a lot. Jonah is discerning if nothing else."

"Jonah," I said slowly, "is a conceited prick."

"That, too," he agreed. "But he's a good cop."

I tilted my head, sizing him up. "What does this have to do with me?"

He sat down. For the first time, I noticed the small box on the table between us. The cop slid it across the table towards me, nodding.

"Go ahead, open it."

Inside, there was a tiny star-shaped pin made of brass. At its center were four characters: CCPD.

"What the hell is this? A thank you token?"

Pearce's face soured. "Careful, some people would kill to get one of those."

"Great. Thanks, but no thanks." I put the pin back in its box and moved to slide it back. His hand closed over mine, igniting a hot, uncomfortable feeling along my spine.

"Not so fast." He released my hand and I snatched it back, cradling it in a fist under the table. "What you have there is an official seal from the Chalinex City Police Department. Think of it like a free pass should you ever be stopped by the police. It's yours, for life."

"Gee, and all I had to do was almost blow you up. Thanks." I winked at him and reached out for the trinket, examining it more carefully.

"Not quite," he said drily. "In exchange for this blessing, you will be expected to continue in your role as informant and runner. Starting with this letter here, which you will deliver to your postmaster in Puraimura as soon as you return."

I rolled my eyes. "Thanks, but I already have a job."

"And now you'll have two."

When I opened my mouth to protest, he held up a hand, his green eyes blazing.

"Don't you want to see your brother? Forge a better relationship? This is your chance." He waved the letter in front of me. "This letter will make this precinct a required post stop for you for the foreseeable future. Help us, help yourself. It's your choice. But don't forget the people who might be dying if you refuse to work with us."

"Okay, fine," I grumbled, swiping the letter from his hand. "No need to be so dramatic about it."

"Good. Make sure you deliver that letter when you return home. And keep that seal somewhere safe."

I considered a moment, then pinned the star deep within the folds of my hood. "How's that?

"Should work. Just don't lose that jacket."

"Not a chance," I said, rising. "So, if that's all?"

The detective opened his mouth like he wanted to say more, but then he closed it. Nodding, he waved me from the room. I stopped by Jonah's desk but his neighbor said he was out on patrol. Quickly, I scrawled him a note:

Dear Brother, Twin Heart,
Follow the stars and stay safe.
Your Sister, Nikta

And then, I was out the door, hitting the pavement before Lyric Pearce could think to call me back into his domain again. I didn't slow down, my feet gaining speed as my mind spun. How dare he? In one smooth move, he had cornered me into working for him, with him. Into putting myself in danger. It was my own fault; he'd seen how desperate I was to regain some sense of family with Jonah. But forcing a member of the PGPS to do his bidding – in a universe so vast some world's could not be seen even as stars, we postal carrier held a special position. We were, in many ways, above of society. A league of our own. And he had breached our sanctity. My sanctity.

I was furious.

My hand still burned where he'd touched it, seared by his sheer nerve.

He'd corralled me neatly into his trap and who knew where it was going to take me. I'd been so excited to come here, to this cesspool of vice and prejudice. All I'd thought of was Jonah. Well, I'd gotten everything I'd wanted. Already, I missed my old sector, the days I'd spent beating country paths to reach simple homesteads. The people I'd come across had been angels compared to the sleazes here in Chalinex.

I jogged up the steps to the Enso and banged my fist furiously against the door, forgetting its magical wardings. Too late, I pulled back, only to find myself flying down the steps to land hard on my tailbone. The door burst open and Viv stared down at me, trying not to laugh. Of course, she failed.

"Are you okay?" she wheezed, coming to help me stand. "Sorry about the door, it can get a bit uppity sometimes."

"Your door has an attitude?" I asked, getting to my feet.

"Of course," Ava called from above. "Viv placed the wards herself."

"Ah," I said.

"Sorry," Viv repeated, a bit more sincerely this time. "I thought it might teach some of the more uppity regs some humility."

"Or just make them hate us more," I rejoined.

"Meh. The door only reacts this way to someone who brings anger with them to the Enso. So... What set you on fire?"

I blanched, not liking how well she'd read me. "Nothing big. I'm just feeling a little put out, is all." We met Ava at the top of the stairs and followed her inside. "Detective Pierce is forcing me to work with him indefinitely. He's sent a letter to my boss ordering her to keep the precinct on my route."

"Ooh, sounds like someone likes you," Viv sang and I glared at her.

"Hardly. He just wants to use my services."

"Even better," she cackled, wiggling her shoulders suggestively.

"Viv, please," Ava shushed her. "Can he do this? Force you to work for him? If you want, I am sure the Enso-"

"No, please, don't. He's already half-convinced you guys are behind the feed. Let's not give him any more ammunition. Besides, he's not really forcing me, not entirely. He just sort of backed me into a corner, and you know how I hate that."

"Do we ever," Viv drawled, rubbing the tiny scar on her temple where I had once whacked her teen self with a hairbrush for trying to get me to play "mannequin" during one of her piercing experiments.

"Yeah, well, he pointed out that if I do this for him, I can see Jonah as much as I want, so..."

"Ah. So you had no choice, truly. We can only imagine how difficult it must be for you, to be separated from your twin." Ava reached out and squeezed Viv's hand.

"Speak for yourself," Viv joked, then screeched as Ava squeezed harder. "Kidding, I'm kidding. Ai!" She pulled her hand away and massaged it. "Do you see, Nikta?

Everyone thinks Ava is the calm one, but on the inside..." She shook her head ruefully, hamming it up.

Ava rolled her eyes. "Everyone has their limits. Just as Nikta has hers. Detective Pearce will find this out, too, if he pushes you too far. If you need our help, you must come to us. No matter what. Do you promise?"

I nodded, driven silent by her sudden seriousness.

"Good. And do not be so upset. Just think, not only will you get to see Jonah, but us, as well. You have a home here with us whenever you need it."

"Yeah, much better bunk conditions than that drug den you told us about at Jericha's," Viv pointed out.

"Hey, she doesn't live in a drug den," I protested.

"Drug den, druggie boyfriend, whatever. I don't see a big difference. Now, tell us – how did it go with Lyell?"

"Oh, I almost forgot. It was so awful, I think I practically blocked it out."

"Oh no, what happened?" they both asked.

"Well, at first it wasn't so bad. I got past his uppity butler, and it looked like Axel was going to hit on me like any other sleaze. He took me into this room, it was terrible." I paused, shuddering.

"Did that bastard hurt you?" Viv asked, outraged. Her hair took on a fiery aura, and I knew if I said yes Axel's days on Renga would be numbered.

"No, nothing like that."

"Peace, Vivian," Ava murmured, channeling white light into her sister. Viv visibly calmed and I went on.

"Lyell has a whole room filled with exotic cat furs. It was like some sort of trophy room. When he turned his sights on me, I realized he has some sort of ket fetish. I gave him the letter, then thought maybe I could use his interest to get more information-"

"You didn't," Viv muttered.

"I did," I confirmed, feeling stupid for it now. "I said my husband had been talking about the feed and begged me to ask around when I was in town. I thought maybe I'd learn something, but I don't know. Axel totally freaked out, threw me out of his apartment and threatened to report me to the PGPS." My heart raced at the memory. "If he does, I'm screwed. The PGPS would fire me for sure."

"No, they wouldn't," Ava reminded me. "You have Pearce's seal now."

"You're golden," Viv agreed.

"Though that doesn't help us any," Ava mourned. "Axel still hasn't opened his letter."

"And now it sounds like he probably isn't even our guy. I mean, a drug lord with a ket fetish, he should have given you the royal treatment, right? Do you think he threw away the letter, you know, in a rage because you were so inappropriate?" Viv asked. I could tell she was just teasing, but still it stung. I'd never been anything other than the most exemplary of carriers. Now, I was delivering secret spells, spying for the police and blowing up precincts. Suffice it to say that I was feeling a bit low.

"No," I grumbled. He's probably just busy rolling around in that trophy room fondling his cat furs." I stuck out my tongue and faux-vomited.

"Good point. Well, there's no way to know until he settles in to open his mail. You should probably get going."

"Tired of me already?" I pouted.

"Never!" Ava protested. "But the sooner you leave, the sooner you can return. And you will, won't you?"

"Absolutely. If you promise to feed me first."

"Done," Viv grinned. "Come on, you're going to love our cook. You can stock up for the run home, too."

"We've taught Edmund all our family recipes." Ava threw an arm around my waist and drew me to her as we walked. "Just wait to you taste his trujillo dumplings, they taste just like our mother used to make."

"Mmm, I haven't had a trujillo dumpling since Baba passed," I sighed, smiling as I remembered my grandmother, their mother's younger sister. "No one seems to make them anymore, and I never got the recipe."

"Well, you're in for a treat then, because Edmund promised us a fresh batch for today. We'll copy the recipe for you, too," Ava promised.

"Oh, I have the recipe, I just never seem to have the time."

"That's why we have Edmund," Viv said, winking. "Well, that and other things. You'll see."

I must have looked confused because Ava explained further. "Edmund is a wiz at working magic into food. Very handy when we want to sweeten a deal with the city commissioner, or make sure an event goes smoothly."

"Like the gala?" I asked.

"Exactly so. It never hurts to stack the deck a little in our favor, considering."

I knew what Ava wasn't saying. That they needed to stack the deck because of regs like Lyric. They didn't trust us, had made up their minds against the ket before even coming to this planet. One only had to look at the Mudlands to know the city officials were corrupt, that they didn't care about kems or the working class.

The Enso's top mandate was to protect our people. The regs thought they did that by policing us – and maybe the Circle did. Now I was finding out it wasn't above breaking the rules to soften the regs' minds and hearts towards us.

I remembered Rae, the boy I'd saved in the Mudlands, and the conditions he lived in. If the Enso wanted to mess with the same people who allowed such squalor, who was I to judge?

CHAPTER 18

*when all you want is quiet
the world conspires against rest*

The whole way home, I couldn't stop my brain from circling. The Enso. Pearce. Lyell. Nestra. Jonah. The Mudlands. I may have screamed a few times, spewing some rage out towards the heavens. Vowing to stop thinking about any of it.

Failing miserably.

I'd slept fitfully, leaning against my pack under the shelter of a rocky outcrop on top of a mountain. The letters and parcels I'd picked up before leaving Chalinex barely fit in my pack, though few pieces were actually destined for delivery in the old city of Puraimura. Most of the high-priority mail would be sorted and shipped to space via Hokku – Prime simply didn't harbor many of the "right" kind of clientele, something I was becoming increasingly grateful for.

The sight of the home office in Prime put an end to my musings. I'd never been so glad to come in off a run. My heavy pack had begun to feel like it was dragging me down, pulling me under, and I knew the feeling had little to do with its weight. I pulled out my trio of keys, unlocked the steel, brass and bronze tumblers and stepped inside.

"Ohalo, gorgeous!" Paisley Berman's husky voice greeted me cheerfully. Part of me, still annoyed with life in general, wanted to swat at her. The better part of me smiled back at the buxom ket and raised a hand.

"Ohalo, Paisley. How's it going? Feeling better, I hope."

I watched her carefully as she unlocked the security gate, trying to gauge her response. I was pretty certain someone had conspired to get Joe off his sniffing post so they could sneak the bomb through the post, the question was, had Berman been in on it?

She clutched at her stomach, looking queasy. "Oh, Tara's talons," she moaned. "Don't remind me. I had dinner coming out both ends for five days."

For the first time, I had two unsettling thoughts as I flashed back to that day I'd picked up the mail. At the first, I blanched. Berman really probably had been poisoned. The second almost sent me reeling: my boots. Joe had been able to smell them from across the room the last time I'd been here. What if their stench covered up the scent of the bomb when I was leaving that day? What if I really was somehow to blame for Duffy's death?

No.

I couldn't think that way.

I forced a grin. "Sounds fantastic. Lucky Sheila."

"Actually, she got sick, too. Doc Brado thinks it must have been something we ate."

The confirmation did nothing for my own appetite. "Oh yeah? How is Doc?" I asked, trying to change the subject.

"Not bad. Still refusing to retire. Thank Tara, 'cause that intern of his still has a lot to learn. You'd think the PGPS could scrounge up someone better to take over as team medic, but no." She threw an arm around my shoulder as I walked through the gate. "So, young one. Are you up for a night on the town? Sheila and I are planning to celebrate our return to health with a night of heavy drinking, gaming, and dancing."

"You know me," I started, but Paisley interrupted.

"I do, and I say it's time you came out with us. A girl can't live by route and rest alone."

"Actually, I can," I laughed. "But I would love a night out. This last run was a bitch."

"Yeah, I hear they have a lot of our canine kem friends over in Chalinex," she joked.

"They do," I sighed, remembering the Mudlands. "I met some. They were nice. But the route sucked."

I didn't add that I'd be having to do it again.

"Well, at least you weren't in my apartment. I swear, there wasn't enough incense in the world-"

"Girl, please." I held up a hand for her to stop. "Spare me the details. Just tell me where and when the party starts tonight."

"Our place. Twenty-one-ish?"

"Sounds good. I'd better drop this stuff off, I swear, someone must be mailing dark matter, this pack is so heavy."

Paisley eyed me critically. "I don't know as I've ever heard you complain about carrying before. Just what happened on this run, Nik?"

"Long story, best told over beers tonight," I said, deflecting the question.

"Okay," she said, pointing a finger at me. "But you're not off the hook. I want details."

"Trust me, you can have 'em." And I would have the rest of the day to figure what I was going to tell her. I knew I couldn't keep the explosion a secret, word was bound to get out eventually. But I had to keep my new job a secret, too. Still, it rankled to have to lie to a friend, even by omission. Florence, on the other hand, would soon know everything.

I hitched up my pack and strode through to the belly of the beast, the large room that housed the postmasters' desks. Here, everything was sorted and passed along to runners and transports after going through customs. Routes were determined, maps were made. Each postmaster was in charge of a different sector of Renga – intimate knowledge of the terrain was not formally required, but was definitely preferred. Florence had run the lands to the east and north of Puraimura for years.

She was deep in thought when I approached, absently stroking her ear while she chewed on the end of a red pencil, staring at a map. I stood by the corner of her desk, waiting. Finally, she glanced up, her dilated eyes focusing to narrow slits as they zeroed in on my face.

"Nikta, you're back!" she exclaimed, jumping up from her seat and scattering papers to the floor in her rush to come around the desk. She threw her arms around me, then apologized, stepping back. "Sorry. Are you okay? You're not hurt? A detective called from Chalinex, said you'd been involved in some kind of attack against the police, and then the news came through the wire about that precinct getting bombed. That someone died... I've been so worried. But you're okay? Your brother, too?"

Her eyes scanned my face, searching for bruises or signs of distress.

"I'm okay," I said softly, reassuring her with a hand on her arm. "Everyone is okay. Well, except for Detective Pearce's assistant. He died."

"What happened? Tell me everything." She tugged at my hand, leading me away from her desk into the relative privacy of the staff lounge and shutting the door.

"There's not much to tell. A bomb got through the mail somehow – that package you gave me addressed to the precinct, it was intended for Pearce –"

"What? No! He didn't tell me that."

"Yeah, well, he's pretty cagey." I thought for a moment, realizing I wasn't sure if I respected or resented him for that. "So I had just delivered the package and was talking to Jonah when the damn thing went off. Knocked us clear across the room, but we were lucky – The cop who opened it lost most of his face. His name was Duffy. Died instantly, so there's that, I guess."

"Tara's talons, you could have been killed!"

"Maybe. I'm not sure... I think the package might have been cloaked with magic. It might have even been keyed to non-kets. But there's no way to really know. Anyhow, the bomb went off, and Lyric decided I was a threat-"

"Lyric?" Florence asked, confused.

"Detective Pearce," I said. "He thought I had brought in the bomb on purpose, took me in for questioning."

"Well, you must have convinced him otherwise. When he called to inform me the cops wanted to co-opt one of our runners, I was reluctant to give my permission, but what could I do? He was pretty clear when he reminded me that local laws supersede those of GalCon or any PGPS regulations."

"I can imagine. I don't think Pearce takes it well when things don't go his way. Speaking of which, he wanted me to give you this."

I drew out the sealed tube and handed it to her, noting her normally razor-sharp nails had been bitten down, jagged and short.

"Flo, your nails, what happened?"

"You happened, dearie. I was worried sick about you." She shook her head, realizing that she could no longer easily pry open mail with her nails in their current state. Smiling brightly, she carefully lifted the end with her teeth instead. "They'll grow back, don't worry. Just try not to get yourself killed anymore, you hear?"

Then she began to read, glancing several times between the page and me. Her ears twitched angrily several times until finally they flicked back to lie flat against her head.

"That, that," she sputtered, seemingly at a loss for words. "Ugh! How dare he?"

She sprang up, pacing and muttering incoherent words.

"Flo, what is it?" I asked, surprised. "What did he say?"

I couldn't imagine how he had managed to offend her so badly. Instead of answering me, she merely thrust the letter in my face.

Dear Ms. Green,

Due to her ongoing involvement in an open case under the jurisdiction of Chalinex City, Nikta Kozan will be required to check in at Precinct 8 regularly for the foreseeable future. We shall inform you at such time when she is no longer required to do so. Please adjust her schedule and upcoming routes accordingly. I remind you that the PGPS is not above the rule of law of Renga and that compliance is mandatory.

Regards,
Detective Lyric Pearce
Chalinex City Police, Precinct 8

"Ah," said when I had scanned its contents. But I thought he had already talked to you about this?"

"Hardly! He asked if you could deliver a letter for them. One letter. Not be treated like his, his-" She waved a hand angrily towards the paper.

"Spy?" I supplied, trying to be helpful.

"I was going to say suspect," she fumed. "How dare he tell me what is mandatory. How dare he. PGPS employees may not simply be ordered around. We have a sacred duty to fulfill. An oath to uphold. You can't possibly be expected to drop everything just because he is miffed that someone took out a hit on him."

I cleared my throat. "Not that I'm a fan of the arrangement or anything, but in his defense, Pearce actually has me working with him to solve the crime. I'm not a suspect. At least, not anymore."

"But you were, though, right? I knew it." Florence's pacing had picked up speed again. "He probably thinks all kets are out to get him. I know those Chalinex cops, I know what they're like," she hissed.

"Yeah, he doesn't trust magicals, that's for sure."

"But he wants you to work with them? How?"

"Delivering more letters. There's this new drug going around, the feed, and the cops are trying to figure out where it's coming from."

"I've heard of it. A cousin in Kyogamura called last week to tell me her daughter is addicted. She was hoping for some advice, but what do I know about drugs? I was always too busy working to do anything like that. I told her sometimes people just have to hit rock bottom first, before they can stop. They have to really want to give it up, otherwise it won't last."

"Yeah, well, rock bottom in this case seems to be death. You should call your cousin tonight and tell her to keep her daughter away from the mail at all costs."

I tried not to reveal how uneasy her news made me. Kyogomura was another one of the early settlements on Renga, now a sizable city far to the south. If the feed had made it there, was there anywhere safe?

"The mail? But why? You think someone's sending drugs through the mail? That's impossible."

I raised my eyebrows and gave her a long look. "Really? I used to think getting an explosive through the PGPS was impossible, too, but it happened. The feed, it's magical. Undetectable, leaves no trace once someone's opened the letter and taken it in. And it's so pleasurable, people are losing interest in real life, they're stopping eating, wasting away. People are dying, Flo, and it's only just the beginning. The Enso's really worried, I can tell you."

"The Enso? What, are you working for them, too, now?" She laughed. I didn't. "Seriously?"

"Seriously. The CCPD doesn't know though. Pearce doesn't trust us, doesn't trust kets. He thinks the Enso might actually be in on it."

"Well, if it's a magical problem..."

"No way, Flo, I'm telling you, the Enso is spooked. They know the regs won't work with them, though, so they've asked me to keep them in the loop."

"So you're a double agent?" She let out a low whistle. "Our little Nikta, who'da thought?"

"Not me, that's for sure. Trust me, I fought Pearce all I could on this. I have no desire to become someone's firecracker show."

"But you're doing it?"

"I am." I sighed. "This drug is bad, Flo, and it's hurting people. If I can help in some small way, I have to. I thought I could just go to the Enso, tell them what was happening and walk away, but they showed me I couldn't."

"Not that this detective is giving you much of a choice," she grumbled.

"I think he just wanted to make sure you didn't stand in my way. He did give me a choice. A small one. This is Jonah's precinct we're talking about, remember? How could I resist seeing my only brother on every run? You know I couldn't."

"That boy, moving away the way he did, leaving you all alone. He doesn't deserve a sister like you."

I laughed. "No, he probably doesn't. But he's my brother, for better or worse. Nothing can change that. I won't let anything change that."

Florence eyed me doubtfully. "If you're sure."

"Sure? Not by a long shot. But I'm doing it." I said the last with more fervor than I felt. Then I remembered. "Oh! Speaking of family – I didn't tell you…"

I launched into a long description of my cousins, decompressing a bit of Florence's anxiety as I regaled her with the sisters' hijinks. Better for her to laugh and remember days long passed than to lose any sleep over the danger I might be in. Buddha knew, I'd been doing enough of that on my own.

Later, when Florence was looking more relaxed and she'd handed me the mail for the Chalinex route, I smiled and hugged her. Kept my smile bright. If it lost a few a lumen for a moment when I glanced at the packets, I managed to cover it with a hug, left as quickly as I could.

I waited until I got home to reopen my pack, dumping my inventory on the table before me. A now familiar scrawl marked a small green tube, sinister in its simplicity. The addressee's name stood out in bold letters, taller than the rest.

Lady Nestra Laroche.

CHAPTER 19

people know your name
like the moon knows the stars' light
and thinks it her own

It didn't bear thinking about. That is what I had told myself twenty times while I got dressed, thrice more as I repacked my bag for the next day's run, and again now as I made my way towards the Bermans' home. In all the excitement, I'd totally forgotten that tonight was a festival day, and it was taking me longer than usual to thread my way between the crowds in the streets.

Tonight was for fun. Tonight was for living. There was no point worrying about something that hadn't even happened yet.

Yet there it was again, that niggling thought. Should I call Pearce or my cousins, let them know I had another delivery for Nestra? It went against every code I had sworn to uphold as a runner. The mail was sacrosanct. Private.

And yet.

What if this was another piece of the feed? Wasn't I honor bound to report it?

If not to the police, surely to the Enso.

And yet.

It could have been a regular piece of mail for all I knew. After all, Nestra Laroche was an important woman with business concerns throughout the 'verse.

And yet.

A shout jolted me out of my head and I jumped to the right to avoid being trampled by several young men running by, laughing. A sign, perhaps, to pay attention to the moment. Forget my worries for the night.

I smiled, stood up straighter. Yes, I could do that. A night of fun would be just what I needed. It was the first day of a new month, technically a work night, but that had never stopped the people of Renga from celebrating. Each lunar month was named after one of the thirteen animals from the Rengan zodiac. A Japanerican mish-mash, our holy systems had grown organically from the folklore and traditions of our ancestors adapting to our environs. As Sakura rose a new month began and the people would welcome the return of the spirits – the blessings of Tara, the auspices of the ancestors, the devas of nature. Matsuri celebrations and solemn shinko processions to the temples were held in the streets. Special meals were served in homes, offerings laid out on altars. And we danced.

Today we welcomed Turtle, reminding us to care for our homes and families, to always carry our love with us. It was a month to count your blessings – and watch your back. Wily, cunning Fox had returned to his den, but that did not mean his schemes had come to an end. Good for business people, but bad for those who had been having troubles. I sighed, wondering what this meant for me. The possibility of improved relations with my brother seemed to be coming at a high price.

I had sworn I wouldn't think of it, so I wouldn't. As I turned on the street of the Berman's humble townhome, I allowed myself to be distracted by the sight of small children chasing each other in a never-ending game of tag. This year, they wore green face paint and shirts stuffed with pillows to mimic turtle shells. I could remember doing the same, holding hands with Jericha as we ran from Jonah and his friends, our parents lighting torches by the front door and decorating our spirit houses with flowers.

I had already left cookies and tea on my own altar at home, praying for an easier month to come. Now, I saw Paisley's wife doing the same in their small yard, lighting small candles in ceramic pots, pouring rice wine into cups and arranging snacks for the spirits.

"Ohalo, Sheila," I called, opening the front gate. "Ready for the new month?"

"Do I have a choice?" She laughed. "Fox did not treat us well, I must say. Hopefully, turtle will shelter us from his pranks." She held a hand to her abdomen, no doubt remembering the sickness she'd endured.

"Do you need any help?" I asked.

"No, no, you go on in. Paisley is still getting ready. I think she's actually taken the spirit of turtle into her; she's moving slower than ever. Maybe you can help her."

"I can try," I said, grinning. I jogged up their front steps, stepped inside and slipped off my shoes, lining them up neatly by the door. I said a quick prayer at a small alcove filled with candles, smoldering joss sticks and feminine godly images, repeating Sheila's request for protection.

I followed the sound of distant singing to find Paisley sitting cross-legged on a tatami mat surrounded by colorful piles of silk and lace, pinning up her hair. She'd settled on a tight green corset bound by golden lace and satin ties. Wide-legged gold brocade pants covered her legs –I'd been coveting the trousers for over a year, ever since she'd outbid me at a benefit auction for the elderly.

"You look nice. I like what you've done with your eyes." She'd circled them in forest green powder in direct contrast to her russet hair, making the deep gold orbs within pop.

"Thanks, it's a nod towards this month's totem. You're not so bad yourself." She gave me an appreciative glance, taking in my short, pale pink sheath, the color an exact match to that of Sakura. A delicate, hand-painted cherry blossom frontlet adorned my forehead. The combination was one of my go-to outfits for

Sakura's kami-mukae, or welcoming of the gods. I dipped my head in thanks.

"Well, I'm ready," she said, gracefully rising, the silken pants falling in molten waves around her ankles. "I suppose Sheila sent you to hurry me up?"

"I would never," Sheila said from behind me, making me jump. I hadn't been paying attention, hadn't heard her come near. I was off my game. "But since you're ready..."

"Shall we?" Paisley murmured to me, linking arms and leading me from the room.

"Absolutely," I agreed.

Outside, the air was hot and humid, a sure sign of the rains to come. As a ket, my higher body temperature welcomed the heat. Just another thing the humans here resented us for – complaining their skin was forever damp, their bodies overheating more easily in the temperate climate of Renga. I stretched and threw my arms around the wives, pulling them close as we walked.

The going was easy on their residential street, but once we'd gone some distance it was a struggle to stay together amid the crowds.

"What's on the agenda," I yelled, raising my voice to be heard above the crashing cymbals coming from a group of twirling tortoises parading by.

"Food! Drinks!" Sheila answered over a trio of giggling girls.

"The Ladybug!" Paisley shouted, pointing towards a side alley. "Come on!"

Grinning, I changed direction and gladly followed their retreating backs. The Ladybug was one of my favorite taverns. They made their own lager in the basement, so the place was always fragrant with malt. One of the oldest pubs on the planet, it had been started centuries ago by a band of widows. Word was, the mining company had given them a hefty settlement after some faulty supports had crashed down and killed an entire squad of workers. Some wives had left the planet, but the rest had joined together and put their money to work for them. It had paid off, too. Descendants of the five families still worked the place, though over the years they'd expanded the business to include a much larger off-site brewery and sister taverns across the planet. All Ladybugs were known as places of refuge and acceptance for kets, a place you could always find a friendly face. The original had a reputation for being a hotbed of rebellious, liberal philosophy – no surprise considering the owners' own distrust of corporations and confederacy. Needless to say, it was a favorite among runners.

We cut through the alley, coming out on an even noisier street, submerging ourselves in the current of bodies until we reached The Ladybug. The crush carried me past the entrance and I had to fight my way back, flattening myself against the wall in a futile attempt to avoid being bruised by an oncoming wave of college students.

Normally, my powers would have risen on their own to create a buffer zone around me; a natural, instinctual response. Unfortunately, my powers were notoriously unpredictable during the early days of each month. Something about the tidal pull of Sakura messed with kets, though some of us felt the ill effects more at other times of the month. Jonah and Jiji had always had problems in the days after it set. Some said it depended on the flow of meridians within the body, how our energies combined with the moons and the planet. All I knew was that right now my powers were at a low ebb and summoning them consciously did little more than dust the sidewalk beneath my feet.

I had to rely on my own tenacity to reach The Ladybug, though the firm pull of Sheila's hand on mine yanking me up the steps didn't hurt, either.

"Finally! I thought you were going to get squished like a bug." Her laugh gave lie to her words. "Come on, let's get out of this circus. Paisley's already inside getting us a table."

The tavern was more crowded than usual but Paisley had secured us three seats between the kitchen and the stage. The location meant we had to crowd around one side of the table to avoid being hit by the swinging door, but we had a great view of the guitarist singing fold songs on stage.

A waitress scurried over, looking harried with her hair sticking up in all directions, and smiled gratefully when we placed an easy order for three boysen-beers from the tap and a large catch of the day, sashimi style.

It was easy to relax here, easy to smile and forget the craziness of the last week, the crowds outside. The artist on stage was a friend of Paisley's, I'd met him before, Jim or Quinn something or other. He sang like the wind through the woods, like doves at dawn – beautifully. Of love, of sadness, of fame and diminishment. As a poet, I appreciated both the lyrics and the cadence. I leaned back, letting my eyes drift lazily over the crowd, and allowed the music to carry me away.

I saw people I knew, smiled softly with a duck of the head, but I wasn't really present. Not until I saw Stephor leaning against the wall in the back, whispering angrily with a hooded man. I couldn't see his face, but I saw the man's mouth form a fierce scowl before he jabbed a finger into Stephor's chest at the same time his other hand moved in the shadows to stuff something into Steph's shirt pocket. It was a movement so slight, I barely caught it. I wouldn't have, if I hadn't been ket. And then the man was gone, walking towards me before disappearing into the crowd like a phantom. Looking at Stephor's face as his gaze met mine, he certainly looked as if he'd seen a ghost. A very unpleasant one. Then, he seemed to shake himself off and plastered a smile on his face, striding purposefully through the crowd to reach me.

"Nikta, hi," he said brightly, pulling up a chair. "Ladies."

"Stephor! I'm surprised to see you here," Paisley exclaimed. I didn't think anything could tear you away from your family."

He blushed, rubbing a hand over his chest as if embarrassed. Or was he taking measure of whatever the person had placed in his pocket?

Was it money? Was Stephor really being paid to stay away from the PGPS? And why?

"Right. Angie went to her mum's for the festival, they're taking the baby to Tara's shrine, some sort of females only initiation, I dunno. Figured I might as well step out for a bit, too, meet up with some friends." He eyed the room nervously over his shoulder, as he was worried someone might be watching him. "It's good to see you all, I was hoping some of the crowd would be here. Nikta, you're looking good. Heard you had a spot of trouble out there in the big city."

"Did you?" I asked coolly. "I wasn't aware it was common knowledge."

Stephor's face turned an even deeper shade of red. "It's not, far as I know. Flo called me when the shit hit the fan, wanted to know what I thought about my route, if I'd ever heard any whisper of threats. Stuff like that."

"And had you?" I toyed with my drink, pretending I was bored with the topic, but I deepened my breaths, scenting for any hint of fear or duplicity.

"No, of course not," he said.

Liar, I thought. The truth was plain in his pheromones, and I saw Sheila's nostrils widen, catching the same notes of sour milk and rotten oranges as me. And then I heard my name up on stage and a loud whistle from Paisley pulled my attention away from Stephor. She clapped my shoulder and I struggled to catch what she was saying. Stephor was gone before I knew what had happened. Apparently, he'd been taking disappearing lessons from his shady friend.

"Come on, Nikta, don't be shy!" Quinn-Jim was saying. "How about a few lines in honor of our cherry moon?"

"Come on, Jin, give the girl a break, she hasn't even finished her first beer yet," Sheila called back.

It was true, I'd barely touched my drink. I glanced down at the paper by my hands where I'd been idly writing, subconsciously jotting down a haiku. Unfortunately, I didn't have anything useful I could read aloud. The verses spoke of betrayal and grifting, hardly suitable for the night's audience. Before I could brush him off, though, another man's voice called across the room, deep and strong.

"I've some words to say, though I'm just a visitor here today."

Jin's smile widened, and he gestured for the man to rise. "Ah, Kokuma, I didn't want to put you on the spot, but of course you are welcome to come on up. Folks, please give a warm welcome to my cousin, Professor Kokuma Bahn from the White Rocks system. He's on sabbatical searching for the most beautiful sights in the galaxy, so of course I told him he had to come here."

The crowd went wild, cheering and stamping their feet, and the man approached the stage with confidence. He may have been an off-world reg, but he parted the crowd as if he ruled it.

"Mother always said you were my wisest cousin," Kokuma said easily, settling his large frame onto a stool next to Jin on the stage. "I have indeed found much to marvel at here on Renga. Will you play along?" His comment was addressed to Jin, but his deep chocolate eyes were locked mine. I raised my eyebrows and took a sip of my sweet indigo ale, waiting to see where this would go.

Obliging, Jin picked out a slow, pleasing melody. Kokuma smiled and closed his eyes for a few moments. When he opened them, he scanned the crowd slowly, building suspense. If his verse was as strong as his stage presence, we were in for a treat.

moonrise satisfies
heart, eyes, magique – world unknown
brings me to my feet

He stood, gesturing towards the sky, one hand over his heart.

applause! applause! petals pink
spread for me across blue sheets

He brought both hands down, mimicking the fall of cherry blossoms, then parting them before him. The crowd oohed, appreciating his risqué turn of verse and Sheila nudged me in the arm, entranced.

love in the atmos
rains down like fire piercing
my chest, Cupid knows

most holy matrimony
earth, heaven, adoration

His eyes zeroed in on mine and he spoke directly to me. No fancy gestures now, his words punctuated only by one raised brow to mirror my own.

hair, lips, poet fine
how I yearn to make you mine
come sit near, whisper

"Buddha's brazenness! Did he just proposition you?" Paisley hissed, clearly undecided as to whether she should be outraged or amused. I hushed her, and lifted my near-empty glass towards the stage, calling out in a clear voice.

moonlit curiosity
charts starcourse unknown – brazen!

unwary traveler
knows not where he treads, strange lands
Hush! buy me a drink

The crowd whooped and hollered, erupting into laughter and applause. I winked at Kokuma who simply smiled back, his gaze a slow, steady burn. My heart stuttered in response, and I hid my response behind another sip of my beer. He raised a hand and the noise died down.

"You heard the lady, bring her a beer!" Kokuma shouted towards the bar.

Jin clapped him on his shoulder, laughing. "There you have it folks, a marriage of the minds and a battle of wits in true Rengan fashion between two of the finest poets I know. Adelaide, get them both a drink, on me!" He nodded for Kokuma to exit the stage and launched into a moon-themed ballad about turtle and hare.

"Perhaps we should write him a new song, about the bear and the tiger?" Kokuma whispered, his lips just brushing my ear.

Did he know about the sensitive nature of a ket's ears, or was this just normal reg flirtation? Jin appeared to be a normal human at face value, and I presumed his cousin to be the same.

"I don't know," I said, looking up at him. Up close, he was even more massive and solidly built than I had realized, making me feel small, like a kitten. "I don't usually do collaborations." I allowed the last word to roll off my tongue suggestively.

"Don't listen to her," Sheila said a little too helpfully. "She loves working with other poets. It's not often she meets her match, on or off the page."

I groaned. "Please, Sheila, don't help."

Kokuma stood straighter, donning a professional demeanor. "Actually, I have an epic I've been struggling with. Jin mentioned you yesterday, said I should find you and ask for some help. And now, here we are. Perhaps you wouldn't mind taking a look? I actually have the pages on me, in my bag. I go everywhere with them, you know how it is to be a traveler." He looked so sincere, so sheepish, I couldn't resist.

"Well, for a fellow poet in need," I began. "But we'd need a quiet place to work. This isn't really the place."

"Jin's home is over-run with rugrats," he grumbled, and I knew he wasn't lying. I'd heard the girls talking with Jin about his brood before. I laughed.

"If you let me finish my meal, I suppose we could head over to my place. If you girls wouldn't mind?"

"Not at all," Paisley and Sheila said in unison, before breaking into a fit of giggles.

"Good, then it's settled, I'll just get my pack and pay my tab," he said.

I nodded, stuffing a piece of fish in my mouth. Something about his pheromones had made me ravenous.

"Good." He moved away, then rounded back. "Oh, I almost forgot. I should warn you." He leaned down again, his beard tickling the hair on my ears as he whispered something only I could hear. "That little noise you made earlier? I want to make you do that again, and again until the cherry moon sits high in the sky."

I coughed, almost choking on the raw salmon in my mouth. "Um, you do know the moon won't reach peak for another six days?"

"Maybe not, but you will," he promised as he walked away.

CHAPTER 20

moonlight bears down on power
touching – trusting – distraction

Turns out Kokuma really did have a poem to work on. And work on it, we did. In the bath, in the garden, in bed, at the breakfast table two mornings in a row. Finally, I had to put a stop to it. I had mail in my bag waiting to be delivered. If I didn't leave, Florence would have my head. I'd dallied long enough.

Kuma, as I'd taken to calling him, didn't mind. Over the course of two mind-blowing days, I'd come to know that he was nothing if not steady. It was almost impossible to rile him and his stamina – well, let's just say it more than matched my own. Rather than try to cajole me into staying in bed with him another day, the giant had simply scooped me into his lap and asked where we were headed next.

"We?" I'd blinked up at him.

"We. I'm here to walk the planet. Might as well start my journey with the best of guides."

"Mmm. Yes, we can't have you running into any bandits. Poor fools, they wouldn't know what hit them. Whoever named you "little bear" didn't know what they were doing."

Kuma had laughed then, explaining that his mother had named him for the father he'd never met. "A kem. You didn't realize?"

"I thought, maybe... But Jin-"

"A cousin on my mother's side. My father was a trader, there one day, gone the next. She never learned his family name, or home planet, if he even had one."

"That's terrible. I'm so sorry you had to grow up without a father," I said, thinking of my own childhood, how much I'd revered my own pa.

"It was tough when I was little. I found refuge in the rhythm of words. Then I grew, and things got easier."

"I'm glad you kept at the poetry, though. I think you really have something there with your epic. Your university is going to love it. You have an Iliad on your hands, seriously."

"And you? Will you ever publish any of your work? Jin says you are the best poet in Puraimura."

"On Renga, you mean," I teased.

"Well, not now that I'm here..." He grinned, and I swatted him.

"You wish," I'd said, and pulled him down for one last tumble under the kitchen table.

After, we'd packed up, locked the door and hit the road. Delivered some letters at a couple homesteads, Kuma waiting respectfully in the distance each time as I conducted my official PGPS business. Not that that stopped Trigger Benny from peering nosily over my shoulder, trying to get a good look at the hulking man leaning against a tree in the distance.

"Who's that," Trigger had asked.

"PGPS supervisor," I said, improvising. "Conducting route audits, looking to see if they can make any improvements."

"Slowing you down, more's like. I thought you'd be here yesterday," Trigger griped.

"Right, well," I bit my lip, coloring. Then I leaned forward, whispering. "Between you and me, he's a bit of a bear. Constantly on me, it's a real nuisance." I made a face. "Nothing I can do about it, of course. If you'll just sign here?"

The grumpy homesteader signed my pad and I left quickly before I could start laughing.

"What's so funny," Kuma asked when I reached him. "That old man wasn't hitting on you, was he?"

"Old? He's barely fifty. Come on, scamp. Let's get out of here, it's not safe to linger on the roads." I clapped Kuma on the back and led him far down the lane, heading off into the woods as soon as we reached the trail I wanted. Two hundred yards in, I had him backed up against a tree, primed and ready.

He nipped at my neck, groaning. "I'm beginning to think there might be more dangerous things in these woods than any bandits in the lanes."

"How so?" I panted, letting him lift me along his torso, fitting my legs around him as he shifted to pin me against the tree.

"Wild cats, devouring the hearts of men." He paused. "A fellow could fall easily in these woods."

I stilled, wary. "Kuma."

"I know, you're a free agent." I felt him smile against my neck.

"I'm not looking for anything more than today. I can't."

"Can't?" He asked, driving into me and taking my breath away. "Or won't?"

"Can't. Won't. It's all the same. I could never leave Renga. I would never-"

His lips silenced mine, and we let ourselves write a poem without words. I knew how it would end. I was sure Kuma did, too. Still, I reminded him the next morning as we picked our way through the trees.

"When we get to Chalinex, I have real work to do. I can't bring you with me everywhere."

"Dangerous work?" He frowned. "Don't deny it. I can smell your fear every time you mention that cursed city."

"I can't talk about it."

"Again with the cannots." He shook his head. "I won't try to argue with you. But I don't give up so easily, either." He held up a hand when I opened my mouth. "Don't worry, I haven't forgotten my agenda. I'll continue on my travels when we reach the city. And when you don't see me for weeks on end, you won't think you've won. You'll start missing me. And then you'll be glad to discover you haven't seen the last of me."

I smiled. "I'm glad now, on all counts." I reached out and squeezed his hand, picking up the pace. "Now come. If we make tracks we just might reach the city by lunchtime."

"Lunchtime? A real meal with ale and three courses? Now that's a promise I can get behind." He matched my pace step for step, and I sped up a bit more, confident that this was a man who could keep up.

I saw to my promise, and Kuma kept his. I treated him to a hearty meal of dumplings and sautéed root vegetables. We received more than one dirty look from the other patrons – apparently, a dingy ket like me wasn't supposed to be fraternizing with such a fine specimen of a reg, no matter how much road-dirt he had on him. For his own comfort in the city, I was glad he could pass for a reg.

"You won't do me the favor of staying out of the Mudlands?" I pressed him again as we were leaving the restaurant.

"And miss a chance to see the bowels of Renga? What sort of social justice warrior would I be if I passed through Chalinex without bearing witness?"

"Chalinex is bad enough, I'd say," glaring at an elderly woman squeezing past us onto the sidewalk, her eyes bugging out of her head at the way Kuma's hand laid on my arm. But maybe I misread her. Maybe she was part mantis and her eyes always looked like that. I smiled generously and decided to give her the benefit of the doubt. Kuma glanced over his shoulder and frowned at the woman's retreating figure.

"You shouldn't have to put up with that. No one should. At home, our kind are revered for their strength and courage. Woman fight for the chance to wed with a bear."

"I hope you mean that figuratively."

"Mostly," he said cryptically, leaving me wondering what he was leaving out.

"Have they fought for you?" I asked, a tiny surge of jealousy flaring within, my hair standing on end at the thought of him christening a forest with another woman's sighs.

"Mostly," he repeated, grinning as he used both hands to smooth my hair and frame my face. "Now calm, kitten. I'll write to you. You mustn't worry that I'll forsake you for another, whatever my needs."

I swatted his hand away, my lips parting in a feral smile. "Such sweet words to part by. However will I make it through the coming days without you?" I mocked, fanning myself.

"I could stay," he said, utterly serious now.

My heart skipped, and I realized I'd fallen neatly into his trap. And me, I thought, a master predator.

I shook my head.

"No, you couldn't. But I will look forward to your letters." I leaned up into him, offering a final kiss. "Safe travels, Kokuma."

"I'd say the same to you, but I fear more for those whose paths you cross – you'll rend their heart and bruise their soul, Nikta Kozan, magic bearer."

I caressed his cheek and kissed him again.

"Farewell, Kuma." I turned up my hood and dashed off into the rain, unable to look at him for another moment, lest I beg him to stay. It took me five blocks of jogging to realize I was headed nowhere. Turning, I reoriented myself towards the palatial dwellings of Chalinex's upper class and maintained a steady pace until I'd reached the home of Nestra Laroche.

"Shit. Shit, shit, shit!" I muttered. I hadn't wanted to fall for the big bear, but he'd caught my attention and now my head wasn't in the game. A mind muddled by lust and infatuation was not going to do me any good here. I needed to clear my thoughts. Damn if I didn't feel like I'd been the one left behind, when all along I'd been the one pushing him to go. I closed my eyes, taking some calming breaths by the gate.

"Can I help you? This 'ere ain't no place for loitering. Move along, ket-scum."

So much for peace and tranquility. The rude voice forced me to open my eyes.

"Ah, hello Clive. Such a pleasure to see you," I bared my teeth at him, half sarcastic grin, half toothy threat.

"Do I know you? Wot you want here?" he asked, peering at me suspiciously. He was alone at the gate today and seemed the jumpier for it.

"Another package for your mistress. PGPS, remember?" I flashed my bangle at him and his forehead smoothed out.

"Right, I remember now. Well, I darn't leave my post, I'm the only one here now," he explained with an air of self-importance, standing taller. "You'll have to see yourself in. Go straight to the door, jus' like afore. No wandering about, now, don't you go getting no ideas," he warned me as he opened the gate and let me slide past him into the grounds.

"Not in a million years," I reassured him.

"See as you don't," he muttered, still trusting me. Which was fine with me – the feeling was completely mutual.

I jogged away, not sparing him another thought as I darted between the perfectly manicured topiaries, not bothering to stick to the path. Paths were for regular people, and that I was not.

I ran up the steps, not slowing my stride, and knocked on the door, taking the green mailing tube from my pack. This time, the butler wasted no time before ushering me in.

"Quickly, quickly. Her ladyship has been waiting over a week for this package. What took you so long?" he berated me as he led me down the hall.

"Package just came in," I shrugged. "We deliver them as they come. If it's late, it's through no fault of mine or the PGPS."

"Hmph," he snorted and stopped before a closed set of doors. "Wait here."

He knocked gently and stepped inside, closing the door behind him. I could hear murmurings and low laughter, and then he re-emerged, a strange blush staining his cheeks, his hair out of place.

"You may enter."

I barely had time to ponder his discomfiture before he gave me a little shove and slammed the doors shut behind me. More laughter reached my ears, louder now that I was inside the room, and I realized it came from two sources, Nestra Laroche and a long-haired man.

"Ah, hello darling," she sang out, how nice to see you again. So much prettier than the last errand boy. I hear you have something for me?"

The man's head swiveled towards me, hungry eyes devouring, and I froze like prey.

"Lyell." The name escaped my lips in a whisper, unbidden.

"Ah, so we meet again, kitten. Have you changed your mind?" he asked. In his own spectacularly creepy, fetishistic way, he seemed to have forgotten how our last encounter had ended. I decided not to remind him that he'd rescinded his lustful invitation when he'd thrown me out of his apartment in a suspicious fit. Instead, I played dumb.

"Um, sorry, have we met before?" I blinked owlishly at him before moving to Nestra's side. "Special delivery for you, ma'am. Please sign here."

She signed, looking delighted to have received whatever was in the tube, and thanked me before hurrying out of the room.

Leaving me with Axel.

I coughed. "Yes, well, I'd best be on my way. Don't get up, I can see myself out."

"But, must you leave so soon? Why not sit with Axel for a spell? Tell me all about yourself." He reached out, fast like a snake, and pulled me down next to him. I couldn't help comparing him to Kuma: where his hands were cold, Kuma's had seared; where his voice wheedled, Kuma's had rumbled; where his breath soured, Kuma's had been so, so sweet. My stomach rebelled, and I wondered how Axel Lyell would react if I vomited in his lap.

"I really must be going, sir. Please, remove your hand from my knee or I'll have to do it for you."

Instead of heeding my warning, his eyes brightened at the challenge and he lunged towards me, weaving his hands between the fold of my jacket in a bid to do more than I was willing.

"Get off!" I hissed, shoving him back with power and a push. Wind rose up around me, making the papers on the tea table nearby scatter to the floor.

"I'm trying," he drawled.

I scrambled to my feet, maintaining the maelstrom around me, and yanked my pack from where it had fallen on the floor. He laughed but made no attempt to follow me as I backed towards the door. Instead, he calmly smoothed his long hair and collected Nestra's papers from where they'd landed, as if nothing had happened.

I reached the door, turned to leave, but before I could open it I heard his voice, hard and angry.

"What is this?"

Against my better judgment, I stopped, turned, looked back.

He was examining a small golden star, turning it over in his hands, frowning.

I swallowed, remembering Lyric's gift. The token must have fallen off in the struggle.

"CCPD?" Axel glared at me. "You're a cop?"

"What? No! It's an old gift from my brother," I claimed, not wanting to offer a complete fabrication in case he decided to check out my story. "From when he graduated the academy. He got one for everyone in the family. Told me to use it if I ever got in trouble with the law."

"Yeah?" he asked, disbelieving. "A seal like this could get you in as much trouble as it could save you, with the wrong sort of people." He tossed it back at me, sneering.

"Right, well. Good thing I don't know any of those," I laughed, pocketing the trinket. I kept my hands in my pockets, hiding the shaking digits as I backed out of the room.

His eyes narrowed, but he didn't say anything else.

"Ohalo!" I reached the doorway and turned, making my way slowly towards the exit so I wouldn't look like I was fleeing.

Just as I reached the door, a hand clamped onto my shoulder.

"Wait," Axel ordered.

"Look, I already told you-"

"Yeah, yeah, I heard you. You have nothing to do with the CCPD. That's all well and good, but I still need you to do a little favor for me. I have a letter I need to send out to a friend, and here you are, a runner." He waved a folded up note in front of my face, an address scribbled on one side, a staple securing the missive.

"Oh, okay," I said, my shoulders sagging with relief. "I can drop it to sorting on my way out of town."

"No, no sorting. I'll pay you extra to carry it off the books. Just get it there fast."

My brain scrambled. Normally I would have rejected his request – I always followed protocol, and all deliveries were meant to get scanned. But I also needed to prove I wasn't undercover if I wanted to stay off Axel's radar. Quickly, I came to a decision.

"Yeah, alright. But don't think this is going to become a regular thing." I took the letter along with several ceecees from him and put them into one of my pack's side pockets. I sensed no magic under the basic seal, so hopefully it wasn't drugs. I couldn't help but wonder what I carried, what the letter might say.

I barely had time to ponder the answer before Axel jammed some coins into my hand and rudely shoved me from the house.

CHAPTER 21

fear is a tool
continuance is power
ride the wind howling

I landed nimbly on my feet outside and took off doing what I did best: running. Heart pounding, trying to pretend everything was still normal, I dropped off a couple more pieces of mail. Still, Axel's envelope felt like a beacon of criminality weighing in my pack, so I did the only thing I could think of.

I jogged up the steps of the Enso and summoned a hot blast of wind, rattling the doors on their hinges. Gears whirred and the imposing panels flew open. I didn't give the arachnid automaton time to lead me, striding ahead down the hallway.

"Viv! Ava!" I bellowed. "We've got a problem! Viv!"

Ava burst into the hallway dressed in a bare ivory silk shift, her pale skin luminescent in the dim light. "Nikta! Tara's toes, what is it? What's happened?" she asked in a low voice, taking me by the arm and steering me towards the room she'd emerged from. I noted this was a simpler space than the fancy audience room we'd spoken in before. Here, tatami mats lined the floor and pillows circled a large crystalline altar illuminated by dozens of candles in the middle of the room.

"Wait." Embarrassed, I pulled my arm from Ava's grasp, removing my shoes before I could further sully the mats. In my haste, I'd forgotten the most basic of manners, neglected to remove my shoes at the door.

"Don't worry about those," she said, taking them from me and placing them outside the door. "Spider will clean any mess you made. I'm more concerned about what's going on with you. Sit down, and tell me everything."

"What is this place?" I asked, distracted by the flickering candlelights reflecting in the mirrored surface below them.

"My meditation room," she said. "I come here to focus my thoughts. Now, speak."

"I almost got made," I said shakily.

"What, how?" Ava looked at me, clearly concerned.

"I had another delivery for Nestra – not drugs, just a regular letter – and when they let me in, that creep Lyell was there. Nestra rushed off, super happy about whatever the letter said, and he started hitting on me again."

"Oh dear. Are you alright?" she asked.

"Well, sure, I can take care of myself-"

"Ava? You in here? I heard voices." Viv's distinctive hair appeared in the door, her sunny smile. "Nikta, hi!"

"Hey, Viv," I replied. I watched the smile fall from her face as she took me in.

"What's going on? Did something happen? Are you okay?"

"Shiny," I replied, feeling anything but.

"Axel Lyell gave her some trouble this morning, Nikta was just filling me in. Go on, Nikta, tell us what happened," Ava urged me.

"So, Lyell propositioned me again, and I rejected him, again. At first it didn't seem like a big deal but then he came after me, really angry. He found this." I showed them the pin Pearce had given me.

"CCPD? Oh my god, he thinks you're a cop?"

"He did. He was pretty mad. I convinced him it was just a present from my brother, figured some truth was better than a lie. But now he wants me to deliver a note to someone off the books."

"A test?" Viv asked.

I nodded glumly.

"Well, that's not so bad, as far as tests go. Who's the recipient?"

"I don't know," I said, surprising myself. "I was in such a hurry to get out of there, I just put it in my pack and took off." I rummaged through the side pockets and pulled it out. It looked harmless, just a tiny white triangle with a staple at its apex. Then I flipped it over and gasped.

"Otto Torriko?" Ava read the name slowly.

"Never heard of him," Viv said, shrugging.

"But clearly our cousin has. Who is he?"

"Some fringe-dweller I ran into last week. His homestead is totally off-grid in this old quarry, there's not even an access path to get to his place anymore, I think they blasted it out."

"Sounds like a good place to hide," Ava mused.

"But from what?" Viv wondered.

"You think he's part of the drug ring?" I asked.

"Maybe. To be honest, we've been thinking Axel isn't even involved. That tracker you gave him didn't lead us anywhere interesting," Ava said.

"Worse, he's RSVP'd yes to our ball. Now we'll have to endure him for nothing." Viv stuck her tongue out, miming illness.

I snickered. "Maybe you can cast an asexuality spell on him, for everyone's sake?" Then, I sobered. "So who is this Otto guy, and why does Axel want me to deliver a note to him?"

"Sounds like he's just messing with you. A guy like that, he's used to getting his way," Viv offered.

"Still, promise you'll be careful. You don't think he had you followed, do you?"

"No, but so what if he did? It's not like I went running to the cops. Besides, I delivered two other letters first. If anyone was on my tail, this shouldn't look suspicious." I thought about the way I'd blown in their doors. "Well, not too much, anyway. I mean, everyone knows the police don't work with the Enso."

"True," Viv and Ava said at once, both looking sour. It wasn't often they agreed on anything, but clearly the Circle's frosty relationship with local law enforcement was one of those points.

"So what do I do? Deliver it? Toss it? Put it through customs?"

"Hold on. Let me see it." Viv held out her hand, closing her eyes when I lay the paper on her palm. She held her other hand above the triangle and began to swirl one finger. Slowly, the paper rose onto one end, turning in place. She breathed deeply, her nose twitching as if she were sniffing the air.

After a moment, she smiled, releasing the spell. "It's fine. No magic to it."

"How can you tell? The feed isn't detectable. And that bomb-"

"I've been practicing my detection skills, trust me, it's safe. Look, the way you tell it Axel must have scribbled that message in a hurry, to catch you before you left. It's probably just a dick pic or a date for drinks. Deliver the letter. It's not dangerous." Viv handed the note back to me.

"Are you sure?" Ava asked. "Shouldn't we at least read it first? If anything were to happen-"

"She'll be fine," Viv interrupted. "Don't be such a worrywart. If we read it, the paper will be ripped and we'll have to use magic to fix it. And that could leave a trace. Talk about suspicious. Better to leave it alone, deliver it as is. Now, how about you, Nikta. Do you feel better?"

"I think I do, thanks." I put the letter away and hugged them both before rising. "I'd better go. If someone did follow me, as you said, I need to seem like I'm just running rounds. I'll see you soon though, okay?"

"Absolutely! We were telling our boss about you, he said to invite you to next month's gala. You will come, won't you?" Ava gushed.

"A gala? Me?" I groaned. "With the Arch-mage? Do I have to?"

"It'll be fun, trust me," Viv said, linking arms with me as she steered me towards the exit. "And we won't take no for an answer. We've already sent an official invitation through the regular mail, it should be waiting for you when you get home."

"Well, if it's an official invitation," I laughed. "I guess I don't have much of a choice."

"Fab. We'll see you then." She kissed my cheek and signaled for the spider to unlock the doors for me. "Oh, and Nikta?" she called as I bounced down the steps.

"Yeah?"

"Wear a dress."

CHAPTER 22

fall seven times, stand up eight
when one is missing, hearts ache

"I just don't know what to do. I'm worried."

Jericha's eyes were round with worry, even as she nibbled one of the cookies I'd brought.

"And the last time you saw him was three days ago?"

"More, now. It's not like Reno to stay away for so long."

"You don't think maybe he found some girls to hook up with?" I suggested, remembering how the themes of his favorite feed-induced dreams.

"No, no way. He talks a big game, but he's actually not much of a player. And he would have checked in with me by now, or at least called Jesse to brag. He hasn't even shown up for work: I asked. He knows I worry, he would have called me," she insisted.

"Damn." I put down my beer and reached for another cookie. "You don't think he's overdosed, you know, on the feed?"

"That's what I'm scared of. But he usually comes home to use."

"What did the police say?" I asked.

"I haven't called them," she confessed in a whisper.

"What! Why not? Jericha, you need to call them. What if he's in trouble?"

"But that's the thing, the feed. He's a user, Nikta. What if me calling the police is what gets him in trouble?"

"Better that than lying in a ditch somewhere, don't you think?"

Jericha swallowed. "I guess. I don't know."

"Look, if you're not sure, we can give it one more night. If he doesn't come home by morning, you can come with me to check in with Jonah at Precinct 8. Maybe he can do some checking without raising any red flags, okay? And if Reno gets mad later, you can always just say you were talking to an old friend, that you never meant to get him in trouble. You know?"

"I could do that." Her ears had perked up the moment I'd mentioned Jonah, and I knew she'd be planning what to say to him for the rest of the night. She had always had a thing for my brother, much as she'd tried to hide it from me over the years. Considering his stance on all things ket, she'd never had a chance. Deep down, I was sure she knew that, so I'd never warned her off. I wasn't going to start now. Besides, Jonah had always saved the worst of his attitude for family – as a cop, I was sure he'd do his best to help Jericha.

"Good, it's settled then. Now tell me about the good parts of your week. Anything fabulous happen since the last time I saw you?"

She snorted. "Here? Not likely. Jesse's been working like a dog and my boss just had a baby so I've been working long hours, too. What about you?"

I thought about Kokuma and blushed, remembering.

"Oh my gods! Nikta, you beast! You've been holding out on me! What's happened? You've met someone, I can tell."

"Sort of. Remember Jin Black?"

"That musician that plays at The Ladybug? You didn't!"

I shook my head, laughing. "No, I didn't. But I did meet his cousin, a professor."

Jericha giggled. "A professor? My word, Nikta, that sounds edifying."

I swatted her. "He's not like that. His name is Kokuma Bahn, and he's visiting Renga on sabbatical. Some kind of poet's walk-about."

"By Tara's grace, be still my heart," she teased, clasping her hands over her heart. "He's a poet?"

I blushed even harder. "Yes."

"You've found your heart match!" she squealed, breaking the tension. I laughed.

"I wouldn't go that far. But I like him. He's a kem… bear."

Her lips pursed on a low whistle. "A bear, huh? Are they everything people say?"

"This one was. But he's gone now. We spent the last several days together, in my apartment, traveling the wilds. That's all."

"Mmm-hmm. I'm sure. Well, you'll see him again though, right?"

"Maybe. He promised to write me." I thought about his last words. "Actually, he wanted to stay," I admitted.

"What? And you sent him away? If I didn't know you better, I'd say you were a cold one, Nikta Kozan."

"I know. I almost didn't. But I have so much going on right now-" I broke off, remembering that I couldn't tell Jericha anything about my new side work.

"Like what? All work and no play makes kittens dull, you know." Absently, she began nibbling another cookie.

"I know," I said. "You're right. I guess I'm just not ready to settle down, you know me."

"Boy, do I ever. You know, not everyone you love will leave you, Nikta. Look at me, we're still friends."

"Friends living cities away."

"Friends forever," she vowed. "No matter the distance. We're family. Speaking of which – I have some money I was going to send back to my mom. You think you could carry it?"

"Absolutely. You know how I feel about your mom."

"Great!" She jumped to her feet and padded lightly to her room. In moments, she'd returned, a thick envelope in hand. "It's for her birthday. She won't take anything from me otherwise, so I save up for special occasions. Then she has to accept it, face-saving, you know."

"Yeah, she's pretty proud, your mom. She's doing well though, right?" I knew she'd recently retired from teaching at the high school.

"Not bad. You know she'd never complain, even after Pop left to "find himself" in space," Jericha said sourly, using air quotes. "But her teacher's pension is pretty small, and she told me she's been doing piece-work to keep busy. Sewing odds and ends for people, minor upholstery work, that sort of thing."

"That doesn't sound bad. She always was great at that stuff." It was how Jericha had learned to sew.

"I guess. I worry that she's having a hard time making ends meet. Our apartment was small for a family, but for just one person..." She trailed off, staring at the stars. "I used to wish he'd come back but lately I just hope he has a really good reason for not coming home. I hope whatever he found out there was worth all the pain he caused."

"That's big of you," I said, rubbing her back. "When I think of your dad, I usually imagine his ship losing power somewhere in the black and him suffering a long, cold death."

"Oooh, you're terrible!" She laughed, swiping a tear from her eye. "But yeah. I've had the same daydream, more than once. At least it would explain why he never came back to check on us. You'll see she gets the money?"

"She'll be my first stop back in Prime, I promise. And from now on I'll make sure to check in on her more often."

"Thanks, Nikta, I really appreciate that."

I looked away, finishing up a verse I'd been scribbling on the envelope before tucking it into my bag. "She's practically family. I've been so busy missing my own, I've been remiss. That's gonna change."

Jericha leaned in for a hug. "Thanks, bestie. Now, how about we turn in? I have a long day tomorrow, our lead singer dropped twenty pounds last month and I just found out I need to take in all his dresses before the end of the week."

"Sounds like fun," I said, grimacing.

"You have no idea." Jericha was smiling again, and I knew she'd gone from worrying about Reno and her mother to plotting how she was going to take the dresses from drab to fab. For a moment, I envied her. Up until the month before, my life had been simple like that. How had everything spun so far away from normal, so fast?

CHAPTER 23

moon wild magic
fast words, trickery exposed
evil cause, evil effect

I couldn't get out of Chalinex fast enough. Detective Pearce had been out when we'd stopped by the precinct. I'd left Jericha with Jonah, writing up a missing person report. A quick stop at the PGPS to grab my new deliverables and I was out of there, heading towards Otto's as fast as I could. With Jericha by my side, I hadn't been able to tell Jonah much of what had happened with Lyell, and frankly, I didn't care. I just wanted to get out of there. Chalinex City gave me the creeps. More than ever, I wanted to mend the rift with Jonah, if only so I could convince him to come home, back to his people. Maybe some time with Jericha would remind him of what Puraimura had to offer: friends close enough to call family; being yourself around other kets; and, of course, being near me.

I wondered if I could get Jericha to come back, too. I snorted. Fat chance of that, now that she'd had a taste of the theatre life. Still, I could dream. I mean, we had playhouses in Prime – theatres run by kets, complete with cat-eared casts. We even had a small opera house.

I breathed easier when I left city limits. Reaching the top of a rise, surveying the wilds stretching before me, I pushed back my hood and allowed the fresh breeze to cool my face. With my powers still weakened by Sakura's rise, I'd been careful to hide my heritage on the city streets, careful to avoid any bad blood. But now I was free of the choler and concrete. I could be me. Just be,

I breathed deeply, called for the wind to strengthen and soar, but nothing happened. Typical. Sakura was beautiful as it rose, but until it reached its peak I wouldn't have much control over my abilities. For now, I might as well be a housecat, for all the magic I had. I grinned. A cat who could run. A cat who was free.

So I did what I loved best. I ran.

Stars streaked overhead, a common occurrence whenever Renga transited one of the many local meteor fields. The sky was painted with swirls of pastel blues and crimson splotches, heated gases and stardust splashing the horizon with watercolor washes. Birds sang sleepily, squawking occasionally as I surprised them, my boots hitting the ground without a sound as I dashed between the darkened pillars of trees seeded long ago by my ancestors.

I was ket, and I was happy. No one, nothing, could stop me. Not Chalinex. Not Detective Pearce. Not even my brother.

I ran, not escape anyone, but to find myself.

To be me.

I ran, I slept, and then I ran some more. Eventually, I came to the place I'd been before, the raped landscape of Otto Torriko's homestead. Jagged edges of blasted boulders reflected moonlight like freshly sharpened knives. Shadowed crevices seemed darker than before, and this time I wondered what creatures lurked in their depths. Toxic species had been banned during the infancy of Renga's terraforming, but over the centuries escaped pets had wound their way into our ecosystem. Cobras, scorpions, Komodo dragons, spiders I tried not to think about – they could all be found if you knew where to look. At least the Komodos stayed on the other side of the planet, wild descendants of a zoo gone wrong.

The lair was out of the way, not the first place I should have stopped according to my route, but I'd wanted to get the illicit chore done with post haste. Now, I scrambled down the rocks, nimbly jumping from stone to stone. Normally, I found this sort of bouldering fun, but at the moment I just wanted to make sure nothing jumped back at me. My boots were sturdy, but the textile uppers wouldn't protect me from snake bites.

Reaching the steps, I stared at the huge titanium door and its knocker. The demon head, an ostentatious display meant to scare away ghosts, now looked foreboding. Ominous. Shaking off the feeling, I grasped its lolling tongue and gave three loud knocks.

This time, a man I'd never met opened the door. Days-old stubble covered his face, and his clothes looked like they'd seen just as many days' meals. He stared at me, bored, and scratched his junk.

"Yeah?"

"PGPS," I said, showing him my bangle. "Delivery for Otto Torriko."

"Come inside, I can't be leaving the door open," he said, scratching himself again and barely moving aside to let me in. "Otto's busy. You can wait in there while I go get him."

He motioned to a small study off the main hall. Inside, the room was as strange and hard as the exterior. The walls were carved into the rock, gaslight reflecting off their lightly polished surfaces. The crimson rhyolite ran through black basalt like streams of blood, and I couldn't shake the feeling that I hadn't just grasped the tongue of a demon to gain entrance: I'd entered the body of one. I glanced around the room, trying to ignore the walls, but the stone was everywhere. They'd excavated rocks to carve Torriko's desk, chairs, even a couple of standing torch bowls, their contents burning white hot by each side of the desk.

"Homey," I muttered.

Otherwise, the room was unadorned, the bookshelves empty, only a handful of papers on the desk. Another large demon face had been rendered in relief on the wall behind the desk and I wondered if it was supposed to be protecting Torriko, or cursing his guests.

"Well, well, the cat returns."

I spun to face Otto Torriko, his white hair slightly tamer this time, his glasses still making his eyes seem bigger than life.

"Torriko-san." I bowed my head, flustered, using the honorific without thinking. It was a title few used anymore, outside of school or family. But he'd made me nervous, and he was an elder. A creeper, for sure, but also an elder. If good manners could get me out of here faster, I was all for them. "I have a letter for you, from Axel Lyell."

"Lyell sent me something special post? Why?" he wondered.

"Not special. Off the books," I corrected him. "A favor for Mr. Lyell." I smiled, trying to look sincere, though the thought of doing any favors for Axel made my stomach turn. "Here. You don't need to sign."

He took the letter from me and I began to edge towards the door. "I can see myself out. Have a good day, sir." I watched him scan the letter, hold up a hand.

"Wait." He motioned behind me, and I heard a door click shut. I turned and saw the bearded doorman lumbering towards me. "Hold her."

The man's arms came down on my shoulders, but I was prepared for this. I ducked under his left side, stomped on his foot and jabbed him in the side. My instep connected with hard steel, and I realized he was wearing fortified boots. My punch should have winded him, but instead, he laughed.

"Nice kitty. Easy kitty," he purred.

I reached for my powers, calling up a wind that would knock him and Otto back against the desk and – nothing. Curse Sakura! I was powerless. I could still fight though, and I did, evading his huge, meaty hands, lunging forward to scratch at his face then dart towards the door. I had to get out of here.

I yanked the door open, slipped into the hall, ready to run. I had just reached the exit when I heard another click, softer, more metallic.

"Move another inch and I'll blow one of those pretty little ears off," Otto sneered.

Slowly, I turned, hands up. "Torriko-san, I don't know what you want, but you can't hold an employee of the PGPS. There are laws-"

"Don't you Torriko-san me, cop."

"Cop?" I blanched. "But I'm not-"

"Save it. You know what Axel wrote me?"

I shook my head, trying to look bewildered even as my stomach sank.

"He says you're a cop, told me to enjoy the gift, do what I want with you." He motioned for his guard to hold me, then approached. "Kevin, what do you think I should do with her?"

"Give her to me?" Kevin said hopefully.

"Please, I'm not who he says. My brother's on the force, he gave me a CCPD token as a gift, in case I ever got into trouble. I'm not a cop! Let me go."

"Not a cop, eh? That's what they all say. Even if what you say is true, you are a valuable gift – you could get me out of trouble someday, too. I think I'll keep you." He touched his tongue to his top lip, snakelike. "Let me see this token of yours."

Taking a shaky breath, I handed it to him. "Please, just let me go. I have mail to deliver."

"Mmm. I bet you do. That gives me an idea. Lief!" he bellowed, yanking my pack from my shoulders. I heard footsteps pounding through the hall, nearing, and then the thin man skidded into view, panting.

"Yes, Otto?"

Otto tossed the pack at Lief, the latter barely catching it, clutching it clumsily to his chest.

"Cross the stream to the east and take that several miles away. Dump the contents on the ground, stomp on them. Make it look like there was a struggle, like she was taken by bandits."

Lief nodded, headed to the door. I began to struggle in Kevin's hold, realizing this might be my last chance to escape.

"Keep her still," Otto growled. Kevin's meaty hand encircled my neck, exerting the barest of pressure against my windpipe. I saw light flare through the hall as the door to outside was opened, and then, all was black.

CHAPTER 24

betrayal starts at the roots
branching down for dark star shine

A sliver of light ran along the ceiling where it joined one wall; otherwise, all was black. My head ached and it felt like I was sleeping on a bed of stone.

No, I was sleeping on a bed of stone.

I spread my fingers out against the cool, rough surface. Basalt, hard against my palms. I propped my elbows under me, tried to sit up, and was met by a wave of nausea. My head swam and suddenly I was thankful for the darkness. I groaned, making the pounding sensation worse, and I had a feeling additional light would have been an unwelcome sensory addition.

"Careful," a voice echoed dully, sounding rather far away. Not in this room. "Don't move too quickly. You've been out for two days."

"Two days?" I struggled to rise, propping my back against the wall and fighting a burgeoning headache.

"Yeah, they think you might have hit your head. There was a pretty wicked thump when Kevin dumped you in your room, sounded sorta like a kettle drum cracking."

I winced, rubbing a huge knot on the back of my head, the source of my pain. "Sounds about right." My hair was matted into a hard crust, and I knew I'd been left to bleed unattended. Left to die?

"Who are you? What is this place?" I demanded.

"Ah. Welcome to the guest quarters of Otto Torriko, the newest and baddest drug dealer on Renga. Very finely appointed, don't you think?"

"Guest quarters?" I asked dubiously. Was this guy messing with me? The room I was in was frigid and I shivered, unused to such cool temperatures.

"Sarcasm, babe. Learn to identify it."

"Sorry, head injury, remember?"

"Right, yeah. Sorry, my bad. We're prisoners. Otto's been a bit paranoid lately, thinks everyone is out to get him. He threw me in here just 'cause I wouldn't tell him where I- well, never you mind about that. Anyway, he's losing his mind, I tell you. Been on the feed too much, can't tell the difference between his dreams and reality anymore, if you ask me."

"The feed? He's a user?"

"User? Babe, he's the manufacturer. He didn't used to use much, just enough to check the quality of the merch, you know? But lately... I don't know. What did you do to piss him off? Kevin won't tell me anything."

"You sound like you know a lot about Torriko. You work for him?"

"I thought I did. Had a real good deal going on, too. All I had to do was bring him some roots every few weeks, dug out from my own secret stash, and in return I'd get twice my regular pay and free samples of the feed."

The guy started going on about how he'd probably lost his job now back in the city since he'd been stuck here for days. He really was an idiot. I tuned him out, stretching my muscles. Everything hurt. My head, most of all, but also my bones. Sleeping on cold, hard stone was not kind to the body, even if one was used to catnaps on forest floors. At least nothing appeared to be broken.

"Hey, are you listening in there?"

"What? Oh, yeah, sure. So, you've been supplying a source for the feed? What's the secret? How's it made?"

"Not completely sure. Part of the recipe is magic, and I don't have a lick of that. I just bring him the roots."

"You said that before. What roots?" I stood up, moving as slowly as possible. I walked the perimeter of my room, mapping things out. My eyes had adjusted to the dim light and I could see fairly well, but it was always wise to take stock. The room had been carved from rock, like the rest of the fortress. Small holes had been drilled near the tops of the walls, probably for air flow, and I imagined that was how the man's voice was reaching me. My bunk was a platform of stone that had been left behind when they carved out the wall. There was a wooden bucket in one corner, and a tray of water and crackers by the door. The door itself was wood, heavy but nowhere near as strong as metal.

"I probably shouldn't be telling you," he sighed. "But, since we're probably both dead, I guess it doesn't matter."

"Cheery," I muttered.

"I aim to please," he said, a bit of flirtation clear in his voice. I rolled my eyes. Some guys just couldn't get their heads out of their pants, even on death row.

"You were saying about the roots?" I reminded him.

"Right, yeah." He clapped his hands together and I could hear the rasping of palms rubbing, though whether for courage or warmth I couldn't have said. "My friend, she has this plant. It's supposed to be this amazing cure-all. Super rare, super expensive. But what most people don't know is its roots have some mild hallucinogenic properties, they trigger pleasure centers in the brain when you drink it as a tea. Nobody knows, see, because the plant is so valuable that no one wants to harvest the roots. But you can, if you're real careful."

"And secretive, too, right? Or am I wrong in assuming you haven't been sharing your income with your friend?"

The man on the other side of the wall coughed. "You wouldn't be wrong, no. But she's not into the feed, so I couldn't tell her. She'd kill me if she knew I was helping it get made, thinks it's killing people-"

"It is," I said. "Okay, so we've established you're a sneaking, thieving idiot. Sounds like a match made in heaven with Otto – why are you in here?"

"I told you, Otto's getting greedy. Wants to make more feed, which means he needs more qualitchka, and I can't give him more than I am already. Otto isn't too keen on hearing 'no.'"

"Apparently not." I rubbed my neck, thinking. Was this guy for real? Or had Otto planted him next door to soften me up, get some sort of confession out of me? Either way, the guy sounded like a real rat. I felt bad for whoever this girl was. And then it hit me.

"Reno?"

Silence.

"Reno, is that you?"

"Who's asking?" The voice was shaky now, but the attitude was still there. The same guy who'd boasted about threesomes, the guy who'd been missing for almost what, a week now? He was here.

"Nikta. Jericha's friend, remember?"

"Buddha's balls, Nikta, what the hell are you doing in here?"

"Mistaken identity," I hissed. "Otto's paranoid, like you said. Thinks I'm working with the CCPD."

"Shit! That explains his foul mood," Reno murmured.

For a minute, neither of us spoke.

"Jer's been worried about you, you know. You didn't come home."

"I know. She always worries too much. But this time, I've been worried, too."

"You should be. Torriko's unstable. And who the hell steals from their roommate? Do you know how important that vine is to Jericha, how long they take to grow? It's the only thing she has from her grandmother. How could you?"

"Hey, it's not like I took the whole plant. Believe me, Otto wants it. But I couldn't do that to her. And look where my kindness has gotten me."

"Oh sure, you're real chivalrous. Such a good heart. You know the qualitchka is sick, right? It looks like crap. You can't harvest the roots forever, you know. The vine grows too slowly for that. You're killing it."

"Well, if it makes you feel any better, I don't think we're going to make it out of here alive, so it should survive," he growled.

"Oh, you're going to make it out of here alive, I swear it. Then I can kill you myself." I was mad. More than mad, I was outraged. A gust of wind blew the hair back from my face, kicking up a decades' worth of stone dust with it.

I closed my eyes against the grit and smiled tightly. Two days. I'd been asleep for two days. Long enough for Sakura to reach peak. Long enough for my powers to return. The first day they were back on tap were many kets' strongest of the month, a day some regs feared. It was as if the days of dormancy and weakness allowed our abilities to charge up, ready to burst forth like shoots from seed reaching for the light of Sakura at its zenith.

I drew the coldness of the air around me like a cloak, ducking my head in silent prayer and opening my palms. If Reno had anything more to say, I didn't know. The only sound I could hear was the howling of the wind, shrieking like a banshee as it whistled through the holes in the wall to encircle me. The pressure in the room grew and for the first time in my life I wished that my fur extended past my mane, that my skin could be shielded from the cold and the stone dust pelting my face like a thousand tiny *hari* needles. I'd never liked acupuncture. I exhaled furiously, channeling the pain down my arms, through my hands. Out into my magic. The wind rushed at the door, coalescing into ice around the frame. Tiny popping sounds echoes through the room, and then the rock around the door was crumbling, falling to dust, and the door fell back with a dull thud.

"What the hell was that?" Reno sounded frightened, winded, and I couldn't blame him. I was pretty sure I'd sucked all the air from his room. I stepped into the hallway, gaslights flickering in blinding contrast with the former darkness of my cell. I turned my ears, searching for threats, but heard nothing. The thick stone walls had worked in my favor, dampening the sound of my escape. Or so I hoped.

I approached Reno's cell, the only other closed door in the hall, and examined the locks. A simple series of slide bolts. I could let him out, no need for a key.

Did I want to?

"Hello? Nikta? Are you still there? Are you alright?" He sounded scared, his voice high with nerves. "Talk to me, babe!"

I rolled my eyes. If I left him here, Jericha would probably be mad. At the very least, she deserved a chance to slap him herself. Against my better judgment, I slid back the locks.

Reno took a step towards me, blinking against the light.

"That was you? Your magic? Damn, girl, that was crazy!"

"Yeah, well, today's my lucky day. Or at least, my most powerful one."

"Right, Sakura's high point. Jericha always shows off this time of month, last time she made these fireworks-"

"Save it, Reno. We need to get out of here. But first, I want to send Otto a little message. Where does he make the feed?"

Reno shook his head, stumbling a bit over the threshold of his cell.

"He doesn't. I give him the roots, then he forces some old ket to do it. Never met him, but I heard Lief laughing about it one day. The roots, mixed with a little magic and who knows what else, that's how they do it."

"But you don't know where?"

Again, he shook his head.

"Alright. Well, let's get hunting."

"But what if we run into Kevin? Or worse?"

"I hope we do. I have some choice words for Kevin."

We followed the hallway down a dead end, turned, and reached some stairs leading up. The next floor looked similar, though these empty rooms were filled with books and ornate objects. Treasure, fit for a dragon's lair. At the end of the hall, by the stairs, one door was locked, barred from the outside much like ours. Unlike ours, however, the walls and door had been fortified with calressium. Unbreakable, even by magic.

"Wonder what they keep in here?" I whispered, grinning at Reno. His eyes widened, and he stepped away. "Relax, pretty boy. No need to call up the banshees here."

I slid the bolts back as quietly as I could manage and nudged the door open. Inside, the cell was richly appointed, three times the size of my own. A real, wooden bed lavishly decorated with fur pillows and velvet throws dominated one corner. On the other side of the room, a rocking chair faced a hovering orb of violet fire, while a grey-haired man slumbered in its seat, a book splayed open across his lap. Lit candles and more books littered the nearby desk, along with magical implements, enchanted tokens and one large, moonstone bowl, its milky surface reflecting a sheen of blues and greens in the firelight.

"Two visits in one day, Otto? To what do I owe the pleasure?" The old man rasped, turning slowly.

I gasped, seeing his eyes. Milky white, the irises and pupils were barely discernable, washed out by the haze.

"Speak up!" The man started, his voice shaking. "You're sneaking and teasing won't work on me, Lief." He raised one fist and opened his palm, a ball of purple flame hovering above his hand.

"Peace, old man. You are a prisoner here?"

"I am," he affirmed. "A man came to my house on Bowen Lake two years ago, said he had heard about my mastery over plant magic. Like a fool, I was enchanted by his compliments. He asked me to come here, to tend to his sick master. But it was all a ruse! That scoundrel, Lief, he led me here, to this very room, to rest for the night. And when I woke in the morning I discovered I could not leave. I have been a prisoner ever since."

"For what purpose?"

"Pharmaceutical research, says Torriko. I don't believe him. For months now, we have been making the same thing, the crimson dream, and never is it enough. Never does he tell me how the test subjects are doing, if it is helping them with their PTSD. I fear he is using the drug for something else. Or else, why would he not let me leave? An old man gets tired of the same room, day after day, even a blind one."

"Indeed," I agreed, smiling at his wheedling tone. "And you never tried to escape?"

"I did, once. I didn't get far. I couldn't navigate the piles of rocks outside and that brute, Kevin, he dragged me back. My magic has always been better suited for the garden. Still, I worked what spells I could, made it difficult for him. Then, it hit me. The noises outside, I could tell that we are far from my home. I didn't recognize the birdsongs, or the winds. In that moment, fear got the better of me. Better to live here as a captive, I thought, than to die starving and free, lost in the wilds. But I never stopped praying for my release."

"Well, old man, today is your lucky day. We'll get you out," Reno boasted with more confidence than I felt he deserved. But he was right, of course we would bring the elder witch with us.

"Absolutely," I agreed. "Before we go, though, I must ask – how do you make the crimson dream?"

"That's a secret family recipe, my dear, I cannot pass it on to just anyone," he said, bristling. His pale yellow fur stood on end, and his ears had turned to lay back against his head in displeasure.

"I understand how you feel. But people have been taking too much – they're dying out there. Are you sure Otto can't replicate your recipe?"

"No, why would I share it with him? The boy couldn't work a lick of magic if his life depended on it. No, he was happy enough to have me here under his thumb. Never even asked me for the recipe. Just as well, few could work it, as I told him." The man giggled, a surprisingly high-pitched sound from the elder.

"Listen, I'm working with the Enso, you can trust me. We're going to get you out of here. But I can't take any chances, we can't leave anything here that would help Otto recreate your work."

"The qualitchka he brought me is all gone. Besides that, the only important thing is my enchanting stone, which I always keep here, in my pocket. Even Otto hasn't laid eyes on it." The man snickered. "I told him I can only do my work in private, like the old devil Rumpelstiltskin. I've had him bring me all sorts of other things to throw him off the scent: rosehips, poppy honey, mountain pine boughs. None of them are necessary, but they do combine to make an excellent tea."

"Your years have made you wise," I agreed, biting back a smile, then paused. "I didn't get your name? I am Nikta Kozan, and this is Reno."

"Reno Klein," Reno supplied his last name politely.

"Kozan, Kozan… Any relation to Aang?"

"My father's uncle was named Aang."

"Dull fellow? Very responsible?"

"So I heard. He passed away when I was just a child, in his sleep."

"As one would expect," the man said, nodding. "Aang would never have done anything dangerous, certainly nothing life-threatening. It seems you do not take after him."

"No, I would say not," I said, stifling a laugh.

"Good, very good. You may rescue me, then, Ms. Kozan. Bartholomew Hill, at your service. Keep the noise to a minimum and I will be able to navigate quite well, despite my eyes. It's all in the ears, you know," he said, tapping his lynx-tipped ears, twice as tall as mine and longer-whiskered. "Lead on, younglings."

CHAPTER 25

run, cornered quarry
predators smell fear, not love
a noose that tightens

We had to climb two more levels before we reached a place I recognized as coming off the main hall. I heard some scuffling ahead and peered carefully around the corner. I couldn't see anyone, but my ket ears picked up conversation coming from Otto's study.

"Quick, hand me the feed you halfwit. I have to destroy it before they get here."

"Destroy it? But won't the boss get mad?" Lief's voice wheedled.

"The boss?" Otto growled. "I'm the boss here. Gimme that. Distract the fuzz till I get back. Tell Kevin not to do anything stupid."

"But, but boss!" Lief whined, his voice rising to a shout, but Otto was already sprinting from the room. Pounding down the hallway. Towards us.

Oh no.

I drew back around the corner, looked for a place to hide. Nothing.

"Quick, back downstairs! We can duck into one of the rooms there. Go. Go!"

But it was too late. Just as we reached the lower level, Otto caught sight of us, yelling in surprise. I had no choice. We had to face him. At least down here, Lief and Kevin might not be drawn into the fight

"We don't want any trouble," I said, eyeing the bundle of mail tubes clutched to his chest.

"And I won't give you any." His hair was wild, his eyes distracted. Then, he noticed Bartholomew behind me and snarled. "You're stealing my kitchen witch? You know I'll find you again, right, Barty?"

"You can try." I shrugged. "Then again, it might be hard after I blind you."

Otto blanched. I raised my palm, the air shimmering as I forged a ball of green fire. I could send it towards his face, do what I'd threatened. But I'd been taught better than that. Magic was for defense. I must never hurt someone willfully in cold blood. Such crimes were not only punishable by the Enso, they were inhuman. The very thing regs feared most about us.

I hurled the ball towards him.

He dropped the tubes, protecting his face, and the fire consumed each bundle of the feed as it fell.

"What have you done? You feral bitch! Do you realize what will happen to me now? To you?"

"Um, I'll sleep better at night knowing no one is dying in their dream worlds?"

"My boss is going to kill us both! All of us! Oh, gods! We're all dead. Dead, I tell you. The weak are meat, the strong eat; didn't your parents ever tell you that?"

"Pretty sure I'm not the weak one here, Torriko-san," I said sarcastically.

"You have no idea what you've done. You think you are powerful, kitten? You've kicked the tiger. We'll all suffer now."

Upstairs, there were shouts, muffled bangs, sounds that even Otto and Reno could hear with their unmodified ears. For a moment, we all looked up at the ceiling, wondering what was happening.

"Sounds like Kevin did something stupid," I said, grinning.

Otto nodded, backing up towards the stairwell. "Watch your back," he warned. And then he was gone, pounding up the stairs.

I chased after him, then stopped, realizing he'd continued down, not up.

"Where's he going?" I wondered.

"Secret escape tunnel?" Reno offered.

"Maybe. Or a panic room. We'll let the cops deal with it. Come on." I led the men back upstairs, hoping the enemy of our enemy would prove friendly.

CHAPTER 26

wake from death and return to life
playing deals like cold fishwives

"You there, move slowly! Put your hands up where we can see them!"

I'd just started to step around the corner into the main hall when I heard the shouts. Someone was all kinds of riled up. I wasn't going to test them. I raised my hands by my shoulders, palms up, and shrugged. Once they saw I was ket, raised hands weren't likely to make them feel any better.

I didn't need a weapon. I was a weapon.

I checked over my shoulder to make sure Reno and Bartholomew followed suit. Reno's arms were straight up in the air high over his head and his eyes were wide with fear. It was the most scared I'd seen him yet, no surprise there considering he was both victim and criminal. Bartholomew's hands were up in front of his chest, more like he was saying "please, don't pick me." The old man was pale but otherwise looked relatively serene.

I watched several cops train their weapons on us. No one's hands were shaking, so that was good. I'd heard enough stories about kets making cops nervous to know being innocent didn't always guarantee survival. Never mind the fact that the majority of violent offenders were regs, never mind the fact that we'd invited them into our world, paved the way for them, literally. We were different, so we must be dangerous.

"Stop right there! Not another move!" I could hear the slight tremor that had leapt into the young man's voice, and I knew he'd caught sight of our ket ears.

I sighed and drawled, "Wouldn't dream of it."

"Cuff 'em." Shaky gestured for the other two cops to approach us. "Resist and I'll fill you with holes faster than you can say 'magic'," he warned. "Put your faces to the wall and your hands behind your backs. Now!"

"Charming," I muttered. "No bias here."

"What was that?" he scowled but didn't move any closer.

"Nothing." I caught sight of the female cop smirking as she approached me and I gathered his bias probably extended to the female half of his race, too.

"Look, we don't want any trouble," Reno whined. "Otto and his crew were holding us captive. We were just escaping when we heard the commotion upstairs"

"Good timing, by the way," I said.

"Don't try and play me." His voice rose an octave. "Pina, cuff her."

"Sorry," the girl cop whispered. "He's an ass, but he's my superior. If what you say is true, we'll have you out of these soon enough."

"I get it, you're just doing your job," I said, loudly enough for the guy to hear. "And I was doing mine. I work with the PGPS and the CCPD. See the bangle? I had a token, too, till Otto lifted it."

The guy shook his head like he was trying to get water out of his ears. "Bull. You're one of them. I know it. I-"

"Bucknell, you idiot." A familiar voice tickled my ears. Then I saw him, Lyric Pearce, striding past the guy, heading straight towards me. "Stand down. I told you I had someone on the inside. Do you ever listen?"

"Sir, you never mentioned she would be a-"

"I'm gonna stop you right there," I hissed, "before you say something I guarantee you'll regret."

Bucknell colored and lowered his gun. Still, he kept his eyes on me, glaring. The other cops uncuffed us and I turned to face Lyric.

"Took you long enough," I joked, but he didn't crack a smile. "How did you find us?"

"The token. It's not just a symbol, it's a tracker. Some sisters at the Enso make them for us."

"Sisters..." I repeated slowly, thinking I was going to kill my cousins. Then, what he'd said really hit me. "Wait, you've been bugging me?"

"Bugging you? Not quite. Just following your movements and monitoring your heart rate. We have a linked map that reveals both. Pretty handy, I must say. I figured you were delivering mail out here, but then when you didn't leave and your heartrate was low for so long, I decided to put together a squad. Glad I did, too."

Buddha bless him, the man actually looked like he'd been worried. He paused.

"Are you okay. Did they hurt you? We found your things miles away, looking like bandits had gotten to you."

"I'm fine. These two, they've been here longer. Reno's the friend I asked Jonah to look for, turns out he'd been supplying Otto Torriko with some qualitchka roots to make the feed. And this venerable gentleman," I said with a smile, "is Bartholomew Hill, Torriko's been keeping him prisoner, I'm not sure why." I felt protective of the elder and had decided that his story must be his to tell. He'd been through a lot, and he was still in danger. I worried Lyric might lock him up, blame him for all the deaths from the feed. I couldn't let that happen. It hadn't been Bartholomew's fault, not really.

"Where is he?" Lyric asked, never taking his eyes off my face.

"He's right here. Bartholomew, meet Lyric Pe-"

A muscle in Lyric's jaw twitched as he interrupted me. "No, Torriko. Where is he?"

"He ran down to the cellars, raving about his boss coming to kill us all. I don't know if there's a way out or if he's hiding. I probably should have followed him, but I was more worried about getting these two out."

"You did the right thing. You five, check it out." He motioned for the cops, who had multiplied during our conversation, to head down the stairs. "Pina, get statements from these men. Nikta, come with me."

He led me down the hall towards the exit. We passed Kevin, dead in a pool of blood on the floor, and Lief, sniveling in cuffs while two more officers stood guard over him. I looked around for Jonah but didn't see him. Had Lyric not told him where the team was going, or had Jonah not wanted to come? Maybe he was outside. Maybe I was worrying for nothing.

Thinking about Jonah not wanting to come triggered something in me, and I started to transfer that annoyance onto the detective.

Why had Lyric bugged me? Hadn't he trusted me?

"How could you?" I demanded, stomping past him into the fresh air and whirling to face him. "Did you really think I would betray you? Do you trust kets so little that you can't even trust an officer's sister?"

"Jonah wouldn't be the first cop to have a criminal for a relative," he said matter-of-factly. I bared my teeth at him and he held up a hand. "Relax, Nikta. I do trust you.

The tracker, it was for your own safety. What do you think would have happened if we hadn't followed you here?"

"I would have gotten out. Like I was doing. You had no right to do what you did."

He shook his head. "I had every right. Look, I know you went to the Enso behind my back, but I still decided to give you a chance. I want to trust you, Nikta. I think we can make a good team. I'm not arresting your friend Reno, or that old man. I think that says something, don't you?"

He smiled, and I wanted to believe him. I wanted to trust him, and that made me more angry for some reason. What was it about Lyric Pearce that made me want to swat him and settle down, all at the same time? I wrinkled my nose, decided I didn't want to know.

"You want a prize for good Samaritan of the year?" I asked. "Forget it, never mind. Though Reno, he's pretty hard-headed. You probably should do something to scare him a bit, make him think twice about taking this kind of gig in the future."

"I can do that, if that's what you really want."

"Yeah," I grinned. "And let the lady-cop do it. A little respect for the female race will do him some good. Reno's kind of a pig."

Lyric threw his head back and laughed. "Done. I'm always happy to give something back to one of my own."

"One of your own?"

"My consultants. You are going to continue working with the CCPD, right? We still don't know who was behind the ring: this big bad boss Torriko's so afraid of. It's always good for us to have an ear to the ground, and in your case…"

He trailed off, grinning at my ears, and they twitched involuntarily. I wasn't sure if I should slap him or laugh.

I chose neither, just rolling my eyes.

"Whatever. I've got mail to deliver, and no time for more of this. Besides, Jonah wouldn't like having me around so much," I said, ready to decline his offer. Then, I had an idea. "But if you'd consider promoting Jonah to detective, I think I could see my way to working with you both."

I expected him to turn it down. Jonah was just a beat cop, a newbie, a nobody. It took years to work one's way up to detective, a spotless record, scores of arrests.

"I'll do it." He looked utterly relaxed, but I could hear the smugness in his voice.

"Excuse me?" I said, shocked. I'd thrown out the idea on a whim, and I'd never expected him to jump at it.

"I'll do it. Make Jonah detective when I get back. I was planning on doing it anyway at the end of the year, barring any big mistakes. He's talented, your brother. And having someone who can work their way around the kem community, it's a plus."

"Jonah? He doesn't want to be anywhere near kems."

"Maybe not, but he understands them, which is more than I can say for most of the force."

"So this is some kind of affirmative action thing?" I asked, crossing my arms.

He cracked his neck and rotated one shoulder, looking annoyed and uncomfortable. "Why do you always have to twist my words like that? I meant just what I said, nothing more, nothing less. Not every reg you meet is a bigot and not every cop is on the take. Jonah is a good guy. I think he can help the force do better. Be better. That's all."

"Fine," I said, smoothing the hair on the back of my neck down. "I guess I'll see you both in couple weeks when I get back to Chalinex, then? And you'll get Reno back to Jericha after you've questioned him thoroughly?"

"Absolutely. Jericha is the friend who filed that missing person report with Jonah?"

"Yes, that's her. Jonah knows where she lives."

"Good. It can be his first duty as a detective."

"Oh, he's going to be so pleased." Jericha, even more so, I thought to myself. "Bartholomew Hill, he is ket, which means he belongs to the Enso. I should take him there. Any information they find, I can tell them to send on to you, of course."

"On any other planet, he would come with me. Splitting up the investigation like this, it's bad for business."

"But it's the way things must be done. Don't fight me on this. You'll be picking a fight with the Enso, too, and you don't want that."

"Oh no," he drawled, "wouldn't want to stir the pot. Fine. You can have your precious elder. But you tell those girls at the Enso I want a meeting. I expect full sharing of information."

"That's your deal to work out, not mine. But I'll tell them what you said." I realized he hadn't worked out that Ava and Viv were my relatives. It felt good to know that I still had a few secrets left, at least for now. "Which reminds me – there's someone else you need to talk to. Stephor Crane."

"Who?"

"He's a reg, a post runner from Prime. I took over his route to Chalinex – and I don't think it was entirely by accident." I told Lyric about how I'd smelled Stephor lying at The Ladybug. To his credit, he didn't crack a single joke or act like it was strange to hear someone identifying pheromones. He promised to send someone to check out Stephor's story. I shuffled my feet, not sure if there was anything else to say. "So we're through here? I can go? Because I have to get back to the Enso in the city, and I'm way off schedule as it is."

"We're done here." He stared me down, arms mirroring mine, crossed across his chest. It seemed like he might say something else, but he didn't.

I shook off any lingering doubts and turned to go collect Bartholomew. I paused in the doorway, something occurring to me.

"Lyric, one last thing?"

"Yes, Nikta?" He was right behind me, following me into the room. Somehow, I hadn't noticed, hadn't heard him in my preoccupation.

I placed a hand on his chest, looked up at him.

"You can't tell Jonah his promotion had anything to me. He's very proud. He wouldn't want the job if he knew I helped."

"Don't worry. I understand. No one likes to think they haven't earned their reward. He's a good man. That's what I'll tell him, and I won't be lying. And you'll be needing this."

He reached out, turned over the collar of my traveling sweater. Underneath, he pinned a shiny yellow brass CCPD token. I couldn't tell if it was the same one, and I didn't ask. Maybe he kept a handful of them in his pocket for times like these. Maybe he liked to give them out to girlfriends. No, not that. If there was one thing I knew about Lyric Pearce, it was that he would be a faithful husband to his wife, whoever she was. He was not a man to take any vow lightly.

He turned my collar down in place, patted it, took a step back.

And that was that.

I collected Bartholomew, retrieved my abused pack from one of the cops, and left Reno quaking in his designer club shoes under the double glare of Pina's eyes. I had to help the elder navigate the boulders to leave the quarry, but once we were on regular land he was able to travel as easily as anyone. I found him a straight, long stick, notching one end to create a comfortable hand-hold for the cane before we set off at a brisk walk.

We didn't get far. We'd barely made it a mile before I heard the sound of arguing through the trees. I held up an arm, clotheslining Bartholomew who exhaled with a gentle "Oof!"

"Shhh," I whispered. "Could be bandits."

Bartholomew cocked his head, listening.

"I don't think so. Sounds like women."

"And women can't be dangerous?" I asked, annoyed.

"More dangerous than most. But these two sound harmless enough, assuming they are not Nekomato trying to lure us to our deaths. Sounds like they're arguing over which way to go. Come on, let's go see if we can help."

Before I could stop him, Bartholomew was hurrying away, following the voices. So much for avoiding trouble in the wilds. I fervently hoped the women were not Nekomato as he had joked. I'd never seen the feared demons of the mountain wilds, wasn't sure I believed the legends, but that didn't mean a part of me didn't harbor old superstitions. Some said it was the bite of a Nekomato that had given the first ket his magic. That part, I refused to believe. I would never accept that our powers were something tainted or cursed.

The closer we got, the louder the voices rose, reminding me of sisters fighting.

Not just reminding me.

A familiar echo. Two sisters fighting. Two twins, to be more specific.

Ava and Viv were staring each other down, orbs of ice and flame in their respective hands.

"You just try it," Ava warned, her ball of ice splitting into a dozen shinning slivers, their dagger-sharp points all turning to point at Viv's head.

"Hey, guys!" I called out, worried one of them might actually get hurt. "How about we save the killing for another day?"

"Oh my gods, Nikta!?" Ava's ice melted into puffs of steam and she raced towards me. "We were just coming to find you! Are you okay? Did they hurt you?"

Arms came around me, Viv and Ava's, and I felt warm tears from both women on my cheeks.

"We were so worried!" Viv yelled at me, stepping back. "How dare you get yourself caught like that!"

"Well, it's not like I-"

"You could have been killed," Ava scolded. "Don't you know better than to walk into danger during Sakura's rising?"

"I do now," I muttered. "Honestly, I-"

"If we hadn't been monitoring our CCPD maps, we might never have known!" Viv complained, gesturing wildly. A small fern nearby caught fire and I hurried to smother the flames. "You need to be more careful."

"Right, yes, I'm the careless one," I said sarcastically. "What was I thinking?"

"It doesn't matter now, you're safe," Ava said a little too graciously for my pleasure. "You were rescued? The police found you? We were following them but then-"

"Ava lost the tracker," Viv said, pointing an accusing finger at her twin.

Behind me, I heard Bartholomew let out a howling laugh and I looked over at him, grinning. I'd almost forgotten he was with here.

"You know these delightful creatures, Nikta?"

"Know them? They're my cousins. Bartholomew Hill, kitchen witch extraordinaire, please meet Ava & Vivian Lilamoa, apprentices to the Arch-mage of Chalinex. Ava, Vivien, meet Bartholomew Hill."

"Ah, fire and ice. Beautiful, beautiful," he chanted, kissing the hand of each.

Ava blushed, Viv giggled. "Charmed, we're sure," they said together.

"I was just coming to find you in Chalinex. Bartholomew will need safe passage back to Bowen Lake, along with round-the-clock security, I'm afraid. Otto was forcing him to create the feed."

"Was he, now?" Viv looked at Bartholomew with more respect, and a touch of suspicion. "Wait, isn't Bowen Lake on the other side of the planet?"

"Indeed, I think I find myself far from home. And I don't think I'd be safe there if I returned. Can your Arch-mage help me find a safe haven?" he asked, looking noticeably more helpless and frail than usual. If I didn't know better, I would have said he'd just put on a glamour to gain the sisters' sympathies.

"Absolutely," Ava purred, wrapping an arm around him. "We will take care of you until we find just the right place."

"Perhaps you can teach us a thing or two, while you're around? What do you say, sensei?"

Bartholomew lit up at the prospect. "I'd be honored to teach you girls."

"Not all of us," I laughed. "I'll have to be getting back to my route, I'm afraid. Duty calls. But I'll be back in the city in another week or two, depending on how long my next route is."

"Not so fast," Viv admonished. "We want to know everything that's happened. You can't just drop a charming old goat in our laps and disappear into the wilds without spilling first."

"Yes, Viv is right. We want the whole story," Ava agreed, taking her sister's side for once. "Everything that's happened since we saw you."

"In haiku, preferably," Viv sassed.

"You know what? For once, I think I'm all haikued-out. But have I got a tale for you."

GUIDE TO RENGA
An Appendix

Aang Kozan – Nikta Kozan's great-uncle, passed away in his sleep, dull in death as in life.

Allen – A PGPS Customs Master with stringent procedural standards.

Angel and Charlie Oakley – Mother and son in a nice, middle-income family living in a duplex in Chalinex.

Ava Lilamoa – Twin daughter of Nikta Kozan's great-aunt, making her Nikta's first cousin. Ten years older than Nikta. Apprentice to the Arch-mage of Chalinex. Nearly identical to Vivien, white-haired and dark eyes like coal. Ava is long-haired, calm and cool.

Axel Lyell – Long-haired, low-level sleaze.

Baba – Informal word for obaasan, or grandmother.

Bakeneko – In folklore, a cat who has become a yokai spirit or demon, more of a benevolent trickster than the feared Nekomato of legend.

Bartholomew Hill – Old and blind ket wizard with a penchant for plants.

Bobby – PGPS trainee recruited by Nikta.

Bowen Lake – One of the largest fresh-water lakes on the planet, on the other side of the world from Prime.

Buddhism – Not a religion, but a philosophy of self-improvement, Buddhism honors no deities but aims the enlightenment of the self, the soul. Buddha is considered the first known human to raise himself out of suffering into nirvana, overcoming death and the underworld. After enlightenment, he made it his mission to likewise free humanity from the veil of illusion. Meditation, morality, detachment, and non-duality are encouraged.

Calressium – A silvery teal metal so rare and tightly controlled by the Peoples Galactic Confederation that almost no one else had access to it. Can only be cut by itself.

Carry with Care – The designation for any mail deemed too sensitive for electronic transmission or bulk transport, demanding the use of a Peoples Galactic Postal Service special carrier or post runner.

Chaline – A clay-like substance that heals and nourishes the body.

Chalinex City – Big city to the east of Prime City. Dirty, corrupt, everything modern life has to offer.

Chalinex City Police Department – AKA, CCPD. Only the best and the brightest.

Chimeras – AKA, Kems. GMO-breeds of humans, including any blend of animal DNA with human. On Renga, most chimeras are descended from Japanerican miners who were engineered with panther-DNA for survival purposes. The kems of Renga tend to have magical powers, though some say something in the mines triggered other changes in their DNA to make them more in tune with the quantum field of Renga. Is it really just physics, masquerading as the unexplained?

Clive – Servant to Nestra Laroche.

Doc Brado – Family doctor in Prime City.

Duffy Merritt – An assistant detective at the CCPD.

The Enso – AKA The Circle – A self-governing council for the magical kets of Renga. Ascribes to the ideals of harmony and balance, and that all are connected so there must be no harm. Its symbol is the medicine wheel, a circle made of the four elements (air, fire, water, earth) with spirit at the middle. Each local chapter is overseen by an Arch-Mage.

The Feed – Dangerously addictive drug suspected to have magical origins.

Florence Green – PGPS Sorting Master and Manager of the Carry with Care Program. Prior carrier, now in her sixties. Still keeps her nails filed razor-sharp.

Francine Sumisu – Jericha Sumisu's mother, retired schoolteacher, does piecework now to augment her pension. Husband ran off-world years ago.

The Fringe – a planned community on Renga.

Galactic Credits – AKA credits, ceecees (plural) or cee (single). The e-money used throughout most of the GalCon. Two Galactic Credits are worth five Yendar, the local currency.

Galactic Frequency – The primary method of communication throughout the known universe.

The Gunjabmi's – Pablo and Omma. Their grandson Henry sends home money to help them care for his younger siblings.

Harai – purification and blessing rituals held when the moon Sakura sets and the gods and ancestors leave Renga for a week-long period of holy rest.

Hari –Japanese acupuncture.

Hokku – The smallest and closest of three moons. Just a dull blue rock, really, with a twenty-six-hour orbit. Where transports dock.

Innis McRory – Maeve's favorite nephew. Dark eyes, six feet tall, strong and gorgeous.

Japanerica – Tech-driven trading society from First Earth, a blended consortium of Japan, North America and Greenland that drove much of the original colonization and exploration of distant planets. One of the three major players in the United Galactic Front.

Jericha Sumisu - Blonde hair, small-earred ket. One of Nikta's old friends, now living in Chalinex City. Jericha works as a costume designer for the city's Opera house.

Jesse Tagazzi – Jericha's boyfriend, works in medical sales, dark eyes/skin.

Jiji – informal term for ojisan, or grandfather.

Jimmy Lewis – Maeve and Maury's youngest son, errand boy for Otto.

Jin Black– The Berman's friend, a folk musician.

Joe – PGPS Customs Officer.

Jonah Kozan – Nikta Kozan's twin. Once an Olympic hopeful, now a beat cop. Refuses to use his magic and passes for human. Has dropped his Settler's accent.

Kami-mukae – Welcoming of the gods.

Kevin – Otto's scruffy security guard. Not too quick.

Kems – *See: Chimeras*

Ket – Feline-specific term for Kems on Renga. Most speak with a local accent incorporating slightly rolling r's, venturing into a trill when excited. They also tend to hum their m's. (*See: Chimeras*)

Kokuma Matsui – Jin's cousin from the White Rocks system, an off-world kem.

Kyogamura – Another early settlement on Renga, now a sizable city far to the south of Prime.

Lief – A thin man, serves Otto Torriko. Scared and jumpy most of the time.

Lindsey – Jericha Sumisu's flatmate.

Lulu Wakanazu – Nikta's mother, died suddenly from a blood clot just before Nikta and Jonah graduated school.

Lunar Calendar – Adapted from Japanerican traditions, each month is named for one of thirteen zodiac signs: Thunderbird, Fox, Turtle, Cat, Rabbit, Dragon, Snake, Horse, Deer, Monkey, Owl, Wolf, Pig. The first day of each month there are festivals, offerings and parades to welcome the ancestors and deities back to Renga with the rising of Sakura.

Lyric Pearce - Lead Detective at Precinct 8 in Chalinex City. Warm honeyed skin and pale green eyes, wears a gold wedding band.

Matsuri –Festivals to welcome the gods and ancestors back to Renga when Sakura rises.

Maury & Maeve Lewis – Noodle Shop Owners, old friends of the Wakanazu-Kozan clan. Maeve loves peach wine.

Mrs. Herold – Widowed Homesteader with a predilection for tea and talking.

The Mudlands – A deteriorating and dangerous neighborhood of Chalinex.

Nekokai – Derogatory term for the chimeras on Renga, loosely meaning "strange cat" or "faulty feline." Derives from the old demonic legends of the Yokai, Nekomato and Bakemato.

Nekomato – Monstrous cat demons (yokai) who hide in the mountains.

Nestra Laroche – AKA Lady Laroche. Second Daughter of Vice Consul Tindare of the Spartan Legions of Earth, widow of Lord Aganon Laroche. Entrepreneur with many admirers and suitors.

Nikta Kozan – Ket mage descended from the Japanerican settlers of Renga. Post Runner/Special Courier. Fierce, independent and fast with the underscent of flowers. Follows her ancestral Shinto/Buddhist traditions.

Ohalo – Common Rengan greeting and farewell, generally conveying thanks, appreciation and blessings.

Onkoro Wakanazu – AKA Jiji or Ojisan. Nikta's grandfather, the one who trained her for postal work

Otto Torriko – An unsavory character living in seclusion. Messy white hair, eyeglasses.

Oxby – Butler to Nestra Laroche.

Paisley Berman – PGPS Security Guard. Female, married to Sheila, no kids. Golden eyes, russet hair, curvy figure.

Peoples Galactic Confederation – AKA GalCon or the Confederation. The limited, liberal government protecting the rights of humanoid civilizations throughout the known galaxy. Individual planets retain authority over all matters except those delegated by the central government.

Pepe's Pedecurie – A one-stop shop in Puraimura for shoe repair and foot pampering.

PGPS – The Peoples Galactic Postal Service, and an arm of the Peoples Galactic Confederation. Primary delivery system for packages and sensitive communications on Renga.

Pheromones – Kets can smell many things, including lies. When someone lies, they smell like sour milk and rotten oranges.

Post Runner – Special postal carriers employed by the PGPS for hand delivery of sensitive materials marked "Carry with Care."

Puraimura – AKA Prime City or Prime. The first city on Renga (its name actually means "prime settlement") where the initial mines and galactic offices were headquartered. Now hosts a large concentration of settler's descendants.

Qualitchka Vine – Rare floral source of a prized perfume made by only two perfumeries. The leaves and stalks have curative properties. It takes sixty years to mature; its purple and gold flowers bloom only once before the vine withers away and creates seeds. The seeds themselves are viable only for a short window of time.

Rae – Wolven teen kem from the Mudlands.

Rama– Axel Lyell's young lover.

Regs – Said with a hard G, this is what kems call regular, non-GMO humans.

Renga - Nikta's planet. Despite its lack of a sunlit sky, the weather is mostly warm and humid owing to a sky filled with glowing nebulae and three moons. Originally settled and mined for its Chaline by Japanerican miners. The planet's own EMFs plays havoc with computer tech – making it difficult for modern tech to survive. Settlement and mining were difficult, but achieved. Shuttles must come and leave within hours, giving them just enough time to unload before their nav circuits are fried. Now, the planet attracts many people who are tech-phobic, such as health-nuts, criminals, religious zealots and homesteaders.

Reno Klein– Jericha Sumisu's flatmate.

Sakura – Renga's large pink moon (name means cherry blossom). With a twenty-six-day orbit, its passage marking the months and generally bringing several days of rainstorms.

Settler's accent – The kets on Renga hum their m's and slightly roll their r's, venturing into a trill when excited.

Shari – Mudland bully.

Shinko – Shinto processions to the temples in honor of the gods and ancestors.

Shinto – Ancient Japanese religion that melded with traditional Native American beliefs, incorporating the worship of ancestors and nature spirits with a faith in sacred power in both animate and inanimate things. On Renga, Shinto combines with magic and a strong connection to the elements of nature: earth, fire, water, air and ether.

Spider – Magically animate automaton, greets guests and performs basic tasks for the Enso in Chalinex City.

Stephor Crane – PGPS Carry with Care Carrier, out on extended paternity leave. A reg.

Tara – A feminine bodhisattva, or enlightened one, Tara is considered by Buddhists to be the mother of liberation. She guides humans towards loving-kindness, compassion and empty non-dualistic mind.

Time – Days on Renga are twenty-six hours long and based on Hokku's orbit, while years are based on Unified Galactic Time. Sakura orbits every twenty-six days, and Yuki has an irregular orbit that varies from two to three days. There are 13 months Rengan year, following the zodiac, and each week has thirteen days. Most people work two days on, one day off, with a two day weekend at the end.

Vivien Lilamoa – Twin daughter of Nikta Kozan's great-aunt, making her Nikta's first cousin. Ten years older than Nikta. Apprentice to the Arch-mage of Chalinex. Nearly identical to Ava, white-haired and dark eyes like coal. Viv is fiery and dramatic with short, spiked hair.

The Wilds – The untamed, unsettled forests, plains and mountains of the southern hemisphere.

Yendar and cents – The currency of Renga, used on the street though direct deposits are in galactic credits. Yendar is both singular and plural in form. Five Yendar are worth two Galactic Credits.

Yokai – Shapeshifting demons of Japanese mythology, some truly terrifying and evil, some mere tricksters, and still others, (mostly) benevolent spirits like the Coyote or trickster Fox of North American Indigenous legends. A common slur against chimeras on Renga.

Yuki – Renga's medium-sized moon, white and the furthest from Renga with an irregular orbit. (Yuki means snow, which Nikta has never seen.)

Zenta Road – One of the most dangerous streets in the Mudlands, mail there gets delivered under escort.

Zyzygy – Three-day semi-annual alignment event of Renga and its three moons. A time of feasting, dancing, and fertility rites.

ABOUT THE AUTHOR

Ellis Logan lives a quiet life in New England, obsessing daily over superheroes and the gods of old. She spends her days corralling wild children, playing with lynx-eared kittens and talking to trees. When everyone is settled down and the owls begin to sing, you'll find her typing and munching on dark chocolate while faeries whisper stories in her ear.

Follow Ellis on Facebook, Twitter and Instagram at **EllisLoganBooks**

Leave a Review and

Join Ellis's mailing list at <u>EllisLogan.com</u>

More Books from Ellis

Shades of Valhalla
Fates of Midgard
Gifts of Elysielle
Heart Ward
Song Walker
Dream Tracker
The Warping
The Storming
The Burning
Lost Moon

www.ingramcontent.com/pod-product-compliance
Lightning Source LLC
Chambersburg PA
CBHW021521240626
47154CB00002B/724